B.72

M

Gallison, Kate.

Jersey monkey.

DATE DUE		
APR 02 2012		

The
Jersey
Monkey

Nick Magaracz Mysteries
by Kate Gallison
UNBALANCED ACCOUNTS
THE DEATH TAPES
THE JERSEY MONKEY

The Jersey Monkey

A NICK MAGARACZ MYSTERY

KATE GALLISON

St. Martin's Press   New York

M

3 - 92 BT 1795

Design by Judy Dannecker

Library of Congress Cataloging-in-Publication Data
Gallison, Kate.
        Jersey monkey / Kate Gallison.
                p.   cm.
        ISBN 0-312-07006-3
        I. Title.
        PS3557.A414J4   1992
        813'.54—dc20   91-38194
                                                               CIP

First Edition: March 1992

10 9 8 7 6 5 4 3 2 1

FOR HAROLD AND JOHN

The
Jersey
Monkey

One

The sun was almost up over the east wing of Porcineau Pharmaceuticals. Oscar Willingham, perched high in a tree platform on the hillside to the west, stood up and stretched his arms. Soon the herd would return, passing his stand on their way to the bedding area. Then he could get his buck. He rubbed his hands, clenching and unclenching his fingers. His back hurt. His arms and legs hurt. It was very cold.

The tree stand afforded an excellent view of the valley, the building and grounds of the drug company, the road, and the fields beyond. Lights gleamed in the west wing. Faint sounds of production, steam streaming from the stacks.

Then a moving light caught his attention, zigzagging

1

across the grassy lawn behind the factory. Willingham took his binoculars in his frozen fingers to see what this apparition might be.

A man, small, stooped, struggled across the frost-whitened grass with a spade, a lantern, and a box. His breath stood out in front of him. From time to time he stopped to readjust his burden. Sometimes he would carry the spade and try to push the box, and again he would try to carry the box and drag the spade along behind him. The hunter watched the man's progress with interest until he suddenly heard a rustling in the undergrowth nearby.

He looked down, and twenty yards away he saw an eight-point buck. He paid no further heed to the man with the shovel.

The next Sunday, Tracy Fetz awoke with a bad hangover. She climbed clumsily over the sleeping form of her live-in lover, Roger, and staggered to the bathroom, where the medicines were kept. A brand-new bottle of Wankemol capsules awaited her unsteady fingers. She spilled two of them into her palm and washed them down with water from the tooth glass. At once the headache grew considerably worse, and then she fell dead.

Roger, awakening some time later, rose from the rumpled futon to discover her body on the bathroom floor. It never crossed his mind that Tracy had been poisoned by an over-the-counter headache remedy. If he thought anything—thought was not his strongest talent—it was that she had overdosed on some illicit drug. Horrified, pained, he reached for the Wankemol himself, and swallowed the last two capsules.

* * *

Shortly thereafter Howard Strass, CEO and chairman
of the board of directors of Porcineau Pharmaceuticals, began having olfactory hallucinations.
The smell of bitter almonds haunted him. It started
with a bottle of Wankemol in his medicine chest at
home. He thought he smelled something. Unwilling to
cause further public scandal for Porcpharm (as the
family firm was affectionately known), he took it to
the company lab to be analyzed. They found nothing.
He would lift a sandwich to his lips and suddenly
seem to detect the telltale scent. The sandwich would
return untasted to his plate. His wife and associates
pretended not to notice. But he grew thinner.
He would come home from work and embrace his
wife, and her perfume would seem to smell of almond.
He would think, "She's been poisoned," and start back
in alarm.
After a while his chemists gave him strange looks as
the substances and objects he brought in grew odder
and odder. First it was the Wankemol, of course, but
after that came some almond pastries, then little samples of chip dip, soups of various sorts, aftershave
lotion, and finally his toothbrush—homely, well-used,
the bristles fanned—and a bar of complexion soap
(almond scrub). All with an increasing feeling of
shameful compulsion.
He knew well enough that it was all in his mind; at
least, he knew that it had been in his mind the last time
it happened. But was it in his mind this time? That was
the thing. Simply because he was hallucinating yesterday, did it mean that no one would try to poison him

today? Of course not. In any case the first Wankemol poisonings had been unquestionably real.

At last he admitted to himself that he had a problem. The psychiatrist he visited proposed a long, expensive cure. Howard Strass believed there was a simpler solution: find and incarcerate the poisoner.

The police were pursuing the matter, but with insufficient vigor. The security staff at Porcineau Pharmaceuticals were unequal to the task. Strass's mother-in-law, Hester Porcineau, suggested that he hire her good friend, Nicholas Magaracz, the Trenton detective.

Two

Howard Strass stared down at his feet, and ran his fingers through the strands of hair across the top of his bald spot. He had more fingers than he had strands of hair.

"These attacks on me are really attacks on Porcineau Pharmaceuticals. It's all part of the same thing. I'm sure of it." He was explaining his problem to Nick Magaracz, who was having trouble sorting out Howard's facts from Howard's visceral convictions.

"You have some inside information," Magaracz suggested.

"Yes, and I want to emphasize that this is all in the strictest confidence. Not a breath of it must get out."

"My lips are sealed," Magaracz assured him. *So talk already.*

The CEO folded his hands across his pinstripe-vested belly and stared for a long time at the three pictures on his desk. The middle one was a slim, color-less but vaguely pretty woman, presumably Mrs. Strass, and the other two were well-groomed little girls. At last he spoke: "The poisoner is one of our employees."

"What makes you think so?" asked Magaracz.

"We're sure. The serial number on the contami-nated bottle showed that it came from the shelves of our company store. Not even the police know this."

"Couldn't the poison have been put into the cap-sules after Tracy Fetz got hold of them?"

"That's what we told the police, Nick, but I know that isn't what really happened. I know." Nick's task was taking shape as Howard spoke. Howard wanted him to proceed with the investigation along certain lines, but he wouldn't tell him why. Not for the last time, Magaracz felt uneasy about taking this case.

"Howard, why do you want to withhold evidence from the police? It's unhelpful. It's even against the law."

"It's particularly important right now to preserve the reputation of the company."

Ah. The reputation of Porcpharm was more impor-tant to Howard than the risk to his life. Why should that be? It must be worth money. Porcpharm must be for sale. "You guys selling out?" said Magaracz.

Howard started and goggled at him as if Magaracz had slapped him on the nose with a newspaper. "Where did you get that idea?"

Magaracz noticed that Strass wasn't denying it. "Just a guess," he said. "Everybody's merging these days."

"Well, Nick, I might as well tell you, since you've guessed it anyway. Supraordinate Laboratories in Bergen County has offered to buy us out. Don't mention it to anyone. Do you think that would be relevant to these poisoning attempts, though?"

"I don't know," said Magaracz. "Would they gain anything by killing you?"

"No, quite the reverse. I'm all for it."

"So they wouldn't want to see you dead. Well, who would? Is there anyone very strongly opposed to this merger?"

While Howard rubbed his temples and pondered, Magaracz gazed out the windows. Howard's office sat in the point of a glassed-in angle of the building. On one side could be seen the landscaped drive approaching the main entrance and on the other the parking lot and the hills beyond. Men were working in the flower beds, turning the soil, planting bulbs. A solitary raven hopped on the grass, folding and unfolding his wings, worrying something small and brownish.

Then, suddenly, the light dawned on Howard; his face lit up, his mouth opened, he might just as well have shouted, "Eureka!" But he closed up again, and muttered, "No, no, impossible. Certainly not."

"Tell me the name now, Howard. Tell me now. You might not be able to tell me later."

He said, "It's nothing. Nobody."

Why do they always do that? thought Magaracz. They always did that. Here he was being asked to apprehend a poisoner out of a universe of fifteen hundred Porcpharm employees and Howard had a clue, maybe even the name of the killer, but would he spill it? Not a chance. His inner convictions, yes; these he would urge upon Magaracz with pigheaded single-mindedness. But an actual clue, a name, a fact—!

The woman in the picture smiled out at them, lips parted. Perhaps not so colorless. Her eyes were a deep, lustrous brown. "Does your wife approve of the merger?" said Magaracz.

Howard blinked. "Why wouldn't she?" he said. "My plan is to step down as president, spend more time with her and our daughters. We're going to do some travelling together. How could she possibly object to that?"

Taking a different tack, Magaracz said, "What about a girlfriend? I don't like to pry, but we're men of the world here, Howard." The CEO gave him a funny look. Maybe "men of the world" wasn't exactly the right expression.

"If I had a girlfriend, as you put it, it would hardly be a motive for murder."

"Not even for your wife? I mean, you can't tell about women. Sometimes when their feelings are hurt they can get ugly."

"After all this time?" said Howard. "No. No. Not even remotely possible."

"You want to tell me about the girlfriend?"

"Certainly not. It's irrelevant."

"Well, it's your nickel, as they say, but I feel like I'm working in the dark." He waited for Howard to say something else on the subject. When he didn't, Magaracz said, "Okay. How did Tracy Fetz and her boyfriend get a contaminated bottle of Wankemol from your company store? Neither one of them worked for Porcpharm, did they?"

"They lived in the same apartment house as one of the lab assistants here. There's a substantial employee discount on Porcpharm's over-the-counter drugs, and this fellow was buying Wankemol here and selling it to his friends."

"Is that allowed?"

"It's all the same," said Strass. "But you'll want to talk to him after you get settled in your office. His name is Burton Pollert. The secretary will give you a directory of everybody who works here, so that you can find him, and anybody else you might need to interview."

"Have you done anything about hiring a body-guard?" said Magaracz.

"No, do you really think—? I never go out in public," Howard said. "Except tonight, of course, I have to go to that thing of my wife's at the War Memorial."

"Maybe you ought to hire a couple of guys to look out for you," said Magaracz. "If you really think somebody's trying to kill you."

"Why don't you come?" said Strass. "Bring your wife. Keep your eyes open." He handed the detective a pair of tickets, which he happened to have in his breast pocket. "It may prove to be a very entertaining evening. The *Ballet Mechanique*. Do you like twentieth-century music?"

"Never tried it," said Magaracz.

"Come anyway," said Strass. "I'll feel easier in my mind."

The corridors of the Porcpharm headquarters were not easy to traverse. The halls did not always intersect at right angles. The rooms were not numbered consecutively. To compensate for the eccentricities of the architect who had designed this maze, someone had

mounted maps on the wall every hundred feet or so
with yellow dots: YOU ARE HERE. Nevertheless Magaracz
was glad to have Mary Mavis, the pleasant and moth-
erly woman who was Howard's secretary, as a guide.
She settled him into a spacious window office across
the atrium and down the hall from Howard.

As he tried out the desk as a footrest, surrounded by
the latest and best in office supplies and equipment,
Nick Magaracz ventured to congratulate himself. At
last he had left the employ of the State of New Jersey.
Here at last was his job in industrial espionage, the
break he had been waiting for that would catapult him
into the upper reaches of gumshoe life. If he succeeded
in this endeavor he could go around in the Italian silk
suits that his wife so admired on the TV detectives,
pushing the sleeves up to expose his forearms, and
trade in his lumbering old Thunderbird for a new . . .
Ah, but when his daydream reached this point his
mind began to wander, for in truth he cared nothing
for Italian silk suits—that was a whim of Ethel's—but
he really liked cars. All of them.

The first thing that had struck Nick Magaracz about
Porcineau Pharmaceuticals was how easy it was to
park his car there, out in the country, away from Trenton and the savage competition for parking places that
existed among the state workers, some of whom, it was
said, refused to come to work altogether when the
legislature was in session, for on those days whole
parking lots were closed to all but the politicians. Here
you just drove right in and parked. People even left
valuable-looking stuff lying in their cars, right where
you could look in the window and see it, and no little
cubes of broken glass were strewn around to suggest
that cars could get broken into.

Art Pacewick, his old boss, was steamed when Magaracz quit. Or was he? Maybe it was envy. Maybe secretly he was glad. Now he could get some yes-man to go and work for him, some good paper pusher who could keep track of all the pencils and never drive a state car without filling out the right forms. Pacewick. He was made for the state. He was perfectly happy sitting in his big orange cubicle with the file boxes piled up to his armpits bossing all those guys who said yes.

Space was another thing here, empty space. In Trenton, almost every inch of the interior of state office buildings was stuffed with clerks, records, bureaucrats, Capitol police, and all the necessary impedimenta for running a great governmental apparatus. Here there was space. That big atrium with the huge skylight and all the trees. Those offices. Everybody here seemed to have a real office, with a door and everything, one guy to an office. Some of the offices even seemed to be unoccupied.

For instance Howard Strass's precincts. Before you even got to the part of the building where his office was, before you got anywhere near his secretary, or his head flunkies, you went through a big vestibule five times the size of Magaracz's old cubicle at the state with nothing in it but a Chinese rug, a table, and a lamp. No clerks, no guards, no filing cabinets, no cardboard boxes full of reports from the previous fiscal year.

And there was free coffee here. Around the sixty-degree corner from Magaracz's office was a little kitchen, with a sink, a refrigerator, a microwave oven, a bulletin board, and a Bunn-o-matic coffee maker with hot plates for two pots of coffee. Magaracz promised himself a cup as soon as he finished talking to Burton Pollert.

For the time had come to stop gloating and start fighting crime. The directory the secretary had given him listed a Burton Pollert in the animal laboratories, down in the subbasement. He studied the map of the place in the back of the employee handbook and set off to find him.

Three

A Haitian with a silver shield and a blue uniform guarded the door to the animal labs. He asked for Magaracz's pass and the name of the person he had come to see.

"Burton Pollert," said Magaracz, flipping the plastic visitor's badge at him. As a pass, the badge was inadequate. The guard had to telephone to Howard Strass himself to get clearance. "Security seems pretty tight down here," Magaracz observed, as the guard waited, having been put on hold by Strass's secretary. "What are you guarding against?"

"Antivivisectionist demonstrations," he said. "Hello, Mr. Strass, is it okay to let Nicholas Magaracz into the animal labs? Thank you, sir. Okay, Mr. Magaracz, you can go ahead."

The guard punched a series of numbers into the lock, a square thing like a push-button telephone dial. Magaracz committed the combination to short-term memory for writing in his notebook. A buzzer sounded; the door to the hallway swung open.

He was faced with two more doors now, these with windows in them, chicken wire embedded in the thick glass. Both were locked. One door led to the labs, and the other to the office of Carl Gables, DVM.

Dr. Gables's office was fitted up with the usual furnishings: A desk, a filing cabinet, a bookcase, a computer stand with a terminal and small printer, a large bulletin board over the desk. The bulletin board had only neatly typed schedules on it, geometrically arranged. No funny stuff, no girly pictures, no little cartoon men rolling with laughter and saying, "You want it *when?*" or frogs declaring "I'm so happy I could just shit." No family pictures. None on the desk, either. Apparently Carl Gables, DVM, was a dedicated scientist. On the desk a copy of *The Joy of Signing,* a popular sign-language text, lay open to the middle.

No one was in the office. The lab itself was a forest of cages where brightly-lit stainless steel tables appeared like occasional sunlit glades. There a few white-coated workers toiled. There was a bell; Magaracz rang it.

Far in the back of the laboratory a man detached himself from the ape cages and came limping through the connecting door to Dr. Gables's office to answer Magaracz's ring. The man's left arm was in a plaster cast; a nasty red scar cut across his forehead. From the nameplate on his coat, Magaracz saw that it was Carl Gables himself.

Oddly simian in appearance, Dr. Gables might almost have been one of his own apes. His face was that of a wise old monkey, his eyes round, deep set, and close together, his mouth wide. There were coarse hairs on the back of his hand, even on the fingers.

"What happened to you?" said Magaracz. "One of the apes get loose?"

"Certainly not. Is there something I can help you with?"

Magaracz introduced himself. The veterinarian extended a hand and they shook. Faint smells of monkey and disinfectant. "Howard Strass sent me down here to talk to Burton Pollert," said the detective. "Is he in today?"

"Buddy spends his mornings working for Margaret Gagne upstairs in the chem lab," Gables said. "On the third floor. He's only down here in the afternoons."

Magaracz gazed through the window at the animals in Gables's charge. There were many different species, ranging from white mice in varying stages of hysteria to the sleek ape-creatures languidly regarding them from large cages at the back of the lab. Some of the animals were sequestered behind glass; some were obviously sick. As a veterinarian, was it Gables's job to make them better? Or sicker? What were the ethics of this guy's position?

"You get many antivivisectionist demonstrations down here?" said Magaracz. The vet started and glared, as if Magaracz had called him a dirty name. Touchy. "I was talking to the guard about the tight security," Magaracz said. "He told me it was to keep out demonstrators."

"Security in these installations is standard, for many, many good reasons," said Dr. Gables. "Anything you may hear about the mistreatment of animals in my laboratory is a lie."

Aha, Magaracz thought. A lie, was it? What was the story? He would have to check this out.

So he went back up the three flights of stairs to the chemical lab to find Buddy Pollert. The setup was roughly the same as for the animal labs, with a guard, a vestibule, and two doors, one leading to the lab itself and the other to the office of the head honcho.

In this case the head honcho was Dr. Margaret Gagne, and she was in her office when he peered in, sitting at her untidy desk and smoking. Her ashtray overflowed with unfiltered cigarette butts. She rose and opened the door for him.

"I'm Nick Magaracz," he said to her. "I need to talk to Buddy Pollert. They told me downstairs that I could find him here." Dr. Margaret Gagne was tall, tall enough for Magaracz to smell her breath. Tobacco and alcohol. Her brown hair was brushed straight back and caught with an elastic band. She had penetrating eyes; her brows were dark and almost met. She had a strong jaw. Deep lines creased the corners of her mouth.

She said, "You've come about those people who were poisoned." No smile. Maybe she never smiled. "I can't let you into the lab, you understand, for fear of possible contaminants."

"Is there someplace I could talk to Buddy Pollert? I need to ask him a couple of questions."

"You can talk to him here in my office," she said. "Unless there's some reason why you think I shouldn't hear this."

"Not that I know of," he said.

The thick glass window across from Dr. Gagne's desk gave a great view of the laboratory. People were looking at things, mixing things, writing things down. She beckoned to a guy who was crouching behind a table squinting at a row of petri dishes. He stood up, made a note on his clipboard, and came out. He was stooped, fair haired, pimply, and quite young. Like Gables, he smelled of disinfectants and monkeys. "Something I can do for you?" he asked.

"Buddy, I'm Nick Magaracz. Howard Strass asked me to talk to you."

Dr. Gagne and young Pollert exchanged a glance fraught with private meaning. Pollert said, "Listen, I don't want to say anything about Mr. Strass, but I tested some of those samples myself and I don't think anyone's really trying to poison him."

"But what would make him think someone was poisoning him?"

"I couldn't say."

"Your neighbors, though," Magaracz protested. "They died. Right?"

"Not from Wankemol," he said.

"Well, no," Magaracz admitted, "the papers said from cyanide, but—"

"I knew that couple pretty well. Fought all the time, always breaking up. You want to know what I think, I think it was a double suicide. The police found the Wankemol bottle and right away they wanted to blame the drug company. They had a heavy relationship, you know, heavy. My guess is, they simply preferred death."

Margaret Gagne laughed, a short bark. Sure enough, she wasn't smiling. Laughing without smiling. Well, not everybody could do that. "I take it you don't share this view," he said to her.

She said, "Sorry. It just seems like a lot of melodramatic crap. More likely, they simply thought you were supposed to put peach pits in the quiche. Somebody told them it was the in thing this week."

"You knew them?"

"I knew all I needed to know about them." She lit another Pall Mall from the butt of the one before.

Magaracz went back to the pills. "Buddy, you gave Tracy Fetz and her boyfriend some Wankemol."

"I got things for them sometimes, Wankemol, dandruff shampoo, we make a lot of stuff here and the employees get it really cheap." Nothing unusual had happened to any of the bottles of Wankemol or other products he had taken home, as far as he could remember.

"Did you leave them . . . ah . . . unguarded?" Magaracz pursued.

Pollert seemed surprised. "What's to guard?"

So then Magaracz said, "I wonder if you ever thought maybe the poison was meant for you." Apparently it had never crossed Pollert's mind, but now that the suggestion was made, mixed emotions paraded across his face like the South Hunterdon Drum and Bugle Corps. Last thing he did was to look at Margaret Gagne, and then at the door to the hallway, although no one was standing there, with naked suspicion.

"If you should think of any reason why anybody might want to harm you," said Magaracz, "give me a call. My home number's on this card but you can have me paged here in the building during working hours."

"I don't think there's anything."

"Don't wait too long," he said. "By the way, I found the story of that last big antivivisectionist caper in the animal labs very interesting. But maybe you want me to hear your version of it."

Pollert's mouth hung even farther open. "I don't know what you're talking about," he said.

Margaret Gagne laughed her barking laugh. "So," she said. "Carl has been denying everything again."

"Maybe you can clear things up," Magaracz said to her.

"Mr. Magaracz, I never have told anyone that story, and I never will. You may take his word for it that he walked into a door, which is what he told them at the hospital. Or that he was mugged in the parking lot, which I understand is what he told his wife." She ground her cigarette out somehow in the pile of butts. A few more spilled onto the desk. The hospital. They would have kept some record of this mysterious event.

But probably it had nothing to do with this case.

Back in his office, Magaracz postulated theories. Here was an idea: Howard beat up his head veterinarian, who poisoned all the Wankemol in retaliation. Naw, that was stupid. Here was a better one: Buddy Pollert poisoned the Wankemol himself, having some grudge against his neighbor. Much more probable. Magaracz had found that when murder and mayhem were being done an adolescent was usually responsible. By that he meant anybody under thirty.

Following this line of reasoning, Magaracz checked the lab assistant's address in the Porcpharm personnel files and then drove out to Princeton Meadows to find out what he could about him.

What he found was that Buddy Pollert didn't live there any more.

"Kid moved out two months ago," said the super. "He owed me three months back rent. I don't know where he went."

"He was very friendly with that woman who died,

right?" said Nick. "Like, I heard he was in love with her."

The super snickered. "You heard more than I did, if you heard that," he said. "No, the way I understood it, the relationship was strictly business, and that's all I'm going to say about that, since they're dead."

"What? Monkey business?"

"Drug business."

"He sold them drugs?"

"They sold him drugs. They were dealing cocaine. That was how they could afford this place, and the BMW, and all that audio equipment they had in there, and the Cuisinart and everything."

"Buddy Pollert is an addict?"

"Well, he pays his bills like an addict, that's for sure."

"Wonder where he's living these days."

"If you find out, I hope you let me know."

As he got in his car to return to Porcpharm, Magaracz had a sudden flash of intuition. Buddy Pollert was living with Dr. Margaret Gagne. Of course. Never mind that there was twenty years' difference in their ages, or that Nick Magaracz himself found them both kind of repulsive; you couldn't tell by looking at people who would be attracted to whom. Cherchez whatever, was Nick's motto, and it usually served him pretty well.

Dr. Gagne's address was in his little notebook. It wasn't far. He decided to look it over.

Four

Margaret Gagne's house was a small white clapboard Cape Cod cottage in a neighborhood of other little houses, all with green lawns and well-kept shrubbery. The house had no garage. Knocking on all the neighbors' doors, Magaracz found nobody home but an occasional vociferous dog. Women all worked these days. He took down the names of those who had put names on their mailboxes. Maybe later he would call them and pry into Dr. Gagne's lifestyle.

Well, then. If no one was home, no one would be able to see him breaking into Margaret Gagne's house.

He set to work at a back window, where he could work hidden behind a bush. The window was pinned shut with nails, but he found that by shaking and rat-

21

tling it he was able to work them out. Then it was up with the window sash and into the kitchen.

Two cats appeared and began to howl at him for food, winding themselves hairily around his legs. A can of cat food was sitting out. There was mold on it. Dishes and glassware were heaped in the sink under a coating of grease.

The rest of the house was in roughly the same shape. The living room was full of smelly ashtrays. Silver-framed pictures of a young man in cap and gown and a young woman in a wedding veil adorned the dusty mantelpiece. Dustballs skittered before him down the hall. There were no men's clothes to be found in any drawer or closet. Several drinking glasses reeking of whiskey sat on the nightstand by the narrow, unmade, and unappealing bed.

The picture of Margaret Gagne's private life seemed clear enough. No men, and no maid either. He put the pins back in the kitchen window and left by the front door.

Like Nick Magaracz, Arthur Munsen had recently left the employ of the State of New Jersey to take a job with Porcineau Pharmaceuticals. Munsen had spent the last seven years as public relations assistant to the commissioner of higher education. It wasn't exactly a civil service position, and thus lacked the warm, fuzzy quality of a completely protected job, but it was state work. The governor's term was almost up though, and that meant that the governor's political appointees and their chosen assistants would be on the street pretty soon. Munsen had two options: Go back to work for a newspaper at greatly reduced pay, if he could even find such a job, or go to work for Corporate Amerika. There was always starvation, of course, but his wife was opposed to the idea.

Porcpharm was desperate for public relations talent after the Wankemol poisonings. Quite properly, handling the public's perception of Wankemol was left to the higher-ups; Arthur Munsen's first task was an interview with the biochemist who had developed the new AIDS prophylactic, the drug which, taken daily, would reduce the probability of contracting AIDS, even with moderate exposure.

She was a woman. Women in the work place were always news, he figured, if not hard news; a couple of good pictures, maybe get her to show a little leg—they could probably put together a press release that would be picked up by every big daily in the country. Or anyway for the women's pages.

They arranged for him to meet her in the atrium. He found her sitting on a bench under one of the trees, wearing a white coat, her hands folded in her lap. All of a sudden he realized who she was. It was like getting hit over the head.

Munsen had slept with this woman once. Several times actually. He had a mental image of her in a blue-sequinned bikini bottom and pasties and here she was wearing a lab coat, without makeup, her once-luxuriant hair skinned back till she looked nearly bald. The years (ten of them? fifteen?) had lined her face some, and the body that wouldn't quit was quitting now, but, yes, it was—

"Fleur du Mal," he blurted.

She turned her head slowly, and looked him full in the face. He could see she was deciding whether to confess her true identity.

"Artie, that was my stage name," she said at last. "Nobody has called me that since I got my doctorate and quit dancing." Her voice was huskier than he remembered it.

"What are you doing here?"

"Waiting for you to interview me," she said.

My god! A biochemist! What a waste!

"Well, what are you doing for lunch? Or dinner? You want to go out for a drink after work?"

She laughed at him. "How's your family, Artie?" she said. "How's your wife? I notice you aren't asking me about my kids. They're very well, thank you."

"Are you married?" he said.

"No, Artie. My daughter's married now, but as for myself, I decided some time ago that I was better off without a lot of men hanging around. Without any, in fact." He stared at her stupidly. "So let's get on with this, shall we?" she said.

"This is fate, Fleur," he said. "Meet me for drinks after work. I'll be at the Fox."

"Don't call me Fleur," she said. "My name is Margaret. Dr. Gagne to you. Artie, I wish you all the best, but I don't want to resume our association. I'm here under orders and I have to get back to my lab. So what is it you people want? They said something about pictures."

"Pictures. Right. The photographer will be here in a couple of minutes. Meanwhile, I need . . . ah . . . the complete story of your life."

"The hell you do. And furthermore, if I find out that you have been talking to anyone about the complete story of my life, I will kill you, slowly and painfully. Do you have any idea of the toxic drugs, the pathogens available to a practicing biochemist? AIDS, for instance. How would you like to take that home to Shirley?"

"Fleur! You're threatening me!"

"You bet your ass."

The photographer arrived. Dr. Fleur gave him a few grim-faced poses while Munsen wrote down the schools she had gone to, the awards and prizes she had won, the famous scientists she had studied under. Did she put out for them? He didn't dare ask. She might really mean it about killing him.

When he had enough information to write a news release he thanked her and she went back to her antiseptic lab. Munsen retired to his office, there to sit for the rest of the morning thinking of old times with Fleur, and how to get back into her frillies. Maybe he could blackmail her. Maybe he could give a copy of her threats to some lawyer, to be opened in case of his death. Then he could corner her in the company parking lot and proposition her without fear. But she wouldn't ever kill him. How could she kill him? She always used to be so nice.

Nevertheless, he booted up his word processor and began to compose the following letter:

To whom it may concern,

    This letter, to be opened in the event of my
death, either accidental, violent, or under any sort
of suspicious circumstances, is to inform you of
threats against my life made by Dr. Margaret Gagne,
an employee of Porcineau Pharmaceuticals. Dr.
Gagne has threatened to use means available to her
as a biochemist to take my life if I reveal certain
facts of her past behavior.

If I should die suddenly or with violence or under suspicious circumstances, it is my wish that this letter be delivered to the police.

Yours truly,
Arthur Munsen

Five

Seven forty-five that evening found Nick Magaracz toiling up the steps of the Trenton War Memorial with his wife, Ethel, clinging to him for support and teetering in her best and least comfortable shoes. They were surrounded by the cultural cream of Trenton.

The old place looked great, he had to admit, all lit up with the big white steps and the pillars. You would have thought you were in Washington. Parking places had replaced the green lawns that once surrounded the building (state workers had to park somewhere), but otherwise it wasn't a whole lot different from the last time he was there, ten or fifteen years ago, to see the karate competition.

It started to rain as they were going up the steps, and

ladies in furs and long coats made a rush for the door.
Ethel said, "Hurry, Nick. My shoes are getting wet."
He handed his tickets to a man at the door. Inside, a
poster proclaimed the event of the evening: The Trenton Ballet Company performing George Antheil's *Ballet Mechanique* (and selected works).

Sponsored by the Porcineau Foundation.

Sure enough, here came Hester Porcineau in a long
black dress and a startling display of diamonds.

"Nick!" she cried. "What in hell are you doing at an
affair like this?" Two women, a thin one and a fat one,
came trailing after her. He recognized the thin one by
her liquid brown eyes as the woman whose photograph
adorned Howard Strass's desk.

"You're looking great, Hettie," Nick said. "I like
your hair that way."

"It's a wig, Nick," she said. "I got tired of sitting
around the hairdressers." To the women with her, she
said, "Ophelia, Caroline, this is Nick Magaracz, the
Trenton detective. Nick, I'd like you to meet my
daughters, Ophelia Strass and Caroline Gables."

The daughters smiled, and the family resemblance,
obscured by their Mutt and Jeff builds, became more
apparent. Howard's wife, Ophelia, the thin one with
long, kinky hair, was dressed in brown wispy stuff.
Caroline, in green satin, seemed more upholstered
than dressed. *Gables,* thought Magaracz. Was she
married to the vet?

"A detective!" Caroline trumpeted. "You'll be interested in George Antheil. He once played an entire
concert with a loaded revolver on his piano."

"No I won't," said Magaracz. "I hate guns." Why
these people always assumed he was a lover of violence was a mystery. He felt a sharp pain in his shin,

Ethel shushing him, probably, with the toe of her foot.
Now there was a violent person. "You've met Ethel,"
he said to Hester. "My wife."

"How are you, honey?" the old lady said.

"Good, thanks," Ethel said. "And you?"

"Pretty good," said the old lady, "considering
what's coming."

"Oh, Mother," said Ophelia with an indulgent smile.
"You know it will be wonderful."

"The poster says it's sponsored by the Porcineau
Foundation," Ethel said. "Is this your project, Mrs.
Porcineau?"

"Certainly not," said the old lady. "It's Ophelia's.
She's the foundation's executive director these days.
In fact she and Howard have invested in the show
themselves in hopes of taking it to Broadway."

"The world wasn't ready for George Antheil when
he first wrote this music," Ophelia assured them. "But
times change. He was a cousin of ours, you know. A
very distant cousin, but I do so admire his work. He
was born and raised right here in Trenton."

"Right. They named a high school after him in the
townships," Ethel said.

"Nooo . . . that was another Antheil. But George's
music is really quite wonderful, and *dreadfully* neglected. Wait. You'll see for yourself. Of course, the
dancers are wonderful too. Both my daughters are
spark plugs. They're also doing some other twentieth-
century music."

"You must be very proud," Ethel said.

"How's the gate?" said Magaracz.

"Nothing awe inspiring," remarked Hettie. "But all
the dancers' relatives are here."

Magaracz said, "Where's Howard?"

"He's in the bar," said Hester. "Not looking forward to spending two hours in a monkey suit sitting next to that band."

"What's wrong with the band?"

"The orchestration for the *Ballet Mechanique,*" explained Ophelia Strass, "is very unusual."

Magaracz gave the ticket stubs to the usherette, a preppy-looking high school girl, and she gave them their programs and showed them to their seats. "How about this, Ethel," said Magaracz. "Aisle seats to a major cultural event."

"I don't know, Nick," she said. "With aisle seats you always have to be getting up to let people in and out."

"I better go find Howard," said Nick, but at that moment Howard came into the auditorium through a curtained door down front, wearing the monkey suit, and pushed his way past the fur coats in the first row to take a seat between his wife and his mother-in-law. Hoping Howard hadn't drunk any poison while he was in the bar, Magaracz began to gaze around the auditorium, looking for killers and checking out the fancy paint and gilding of the War Memorial building's interior.

Ethel studied her program, a glossy production with two-color art and photos of all the most important dancers and musicians. There was a four-page biography of George Antheil himself. "Look at this, Nick," she said. "George Antheil grew up in one of those houses down by the Trenton State Prison."

A few more spectators trickled in. From somewhere deep in the building came the sound of an orchestra tuning up.

The houselights dimmed. With a low humming, hissing sound the floor in front of the stage rose up to reveal a sizable orchestra. Large bells, a siren, and an airplane propeller occupied space next to the drums; the propeller was pointing at the seats down front where all the rich folks were. The audience applauded the appearance of the orchestra and its conductor. "Unusual orchestration," Magaracz whispered. "So that's what she meant."

"Shh," said Ethel.

A light shone on the podium in front of the conductor, turning his curls to gold and reddening his ears. He faced the audience and bowed, his features invisible. The curtain opened on a fancy looking set.

For a warm-up piece, the sort of thing they did to cover the hubbub of stragglers, the orchestra played something kind of loud and stark, very rhythmic and not very melodic, with an irritating little theme that played over and over again with almost imperceptible variations. A man came out on stage, a big guy with muscles, walking in time to the beat, and in time to the beat began to do calisthenics, or strike poses. He was wearing a blue chalk-striped suit, not very comfortable looking for the sort of thing he was trying to do, and Magaracz thought, well, so this is twentieth-century music. The audience paid attention respectfully.

Toward the end of the piece, the dancer performed a deep knee bend, splitting his blue-striped suit pants from back waist to front zipper. Luckily he was wearing Jockey shorts.

The orchestra continued playing as if everything were happening as expected. Nobody in the audience laughed. So Magaracz and Ethel didn't laugh either. Later on Ethel told him it was a Statement. But he was never sure.

Then the guy left the stage, still posing, and the

music stopped. Everybody clapped. Some stragglers came in. Ethel said, "Now they're going to do *Dnieper Water Power Station,* by Julius Meytuss."

A snare drum rattled softly, with long silences in between. A xylophone went tinky-tinky. The rhythm was that of a steam locomotive trying to get started on an icy track.

They hadn't got into it but a couple of bars when Nick got something stuck in his throat and started to cough. Okay, so he was coughing pretty loud. It wasn't as though he could help it.

The conductor started whacking the podium with his stick, and the orchestra stopped playing, and then the conductor turned around and faced the audience. "You know," he called to Nick, "if you aren't well, you should stay at home. The rest of us want to hear this music."

"You sold me, buddy," Nick said to him. "I'm out of here." But Ethel grabbed his arm and forced him to sit back down again. Cries of "Be quiet!" "Play the music!" were beginning to erupt from all over the house.

"So you don't like that," the conductor said to them.

"No!" replied the audience, or at least a large part of them, men mostly, by their voices.

After everyone was quiet, the conductor said, "We'll try it again, this time without the noise." He tapped with his stick and the percussionists started up again from the beginning. Some dancers came on, and danced around, waving their arms. Magaracz liked it better than the first piece, but still not very much.

Then it ended, and people clapped. "Is this the intermission now?" he whispered. He wanted to sneak out and go home; Howard looked fine, surely nobody was after him. But it seemed that only ten minutes of real time had elapsed since the first appearance of the orchestra. Before the first intermission, Ethel pointed out, they were going to have to sit through the *Ballet Mechanique* itself.

"Besides," she said, "I'm having fun, sort of. Did you know that George Antheil was known as the bad boy of music?"

"It figures," said Nick.

The offering that followed proved once again that one man's music is another man's noise. The dance was sort of neat; the entire company appeared on stage representing the various parts of a six cylinder combustion engine. Little girls were dressed as spark plugs; guys with big bulges behaved like pistons, including the fellow who had split his pants in the opening number, now wearing another outfit; thin ladies did mechanical looking things. All of it was enormously muscular. The din was horrible, and grew worse. One of the little spark plugs fell down trying to do a leap, and rushed off the stage in tears.

Then they turned on the propeller, and Hester Porcineau's wig went sailing away and away, up into the balcony where the students dove for it like baseball fans after a fly ball.

If Antheil had been alive, and present, and armed with a loaded revolver, perhaps he would have shot the music lovers as they fled from the theater. Or maybe he would have blazed away at the orchestra. The dancers were game, Ophelia and her friends were up for it, but the dentists, pediatricians, students, and aesthetically minded state workers who had come in out of the rain seeking an evening's entertainment were forced to go back out in the rain and seek further. Nick and Ethel started out too, until suddenly Nick heard a commotion—other than the concert itself—and looked over his shoulder at what was left of the audience.

Howard Strass was leaning across the brass rail that separated him from the orchestra pit and being violently sick all over the second violins.

Six

They rushed Howard Strass to Mercer Medical Center, where he was hustled past the patient huddled masses in the emergency waiting room (one of them a youth with a knife sticking out of his back) and taken inside to have his stomach pumped. Nick and Ethel waited for the outcome with Hester and Ophelia.

For some time the women sat wringing their hands and engaging in desultory conversation while Magaracz berated himself for failing in his duty as a bodyguard. In his own defense he had to admit that nothing in his experience had prepared him to keep guys from being poisoned. How do you do that? Taste everything first? Forget it.

The doctor on duty called Ophelia in.

Would Howard recover? Was he dead? Was this the end of Nick Magaracz's long-desired career in industrial espionage? Two more locals dragged their bleeding bodies through the emergency entrance and lurched up to the receptionist's desk. As the receptionist tried to get them to fill out the proper papers, Ophelia emerged.

"He'll be all right," she said. "They'll let me take him home in about an hour."

"What was it?" Hester asked.

"They aren't sure," said Ophelia. "They said there was something in his Porcinox." Howard customarily carried a little bottle of the stomachache remedy, she explained, an over-the-counter preparation made by Porcpharm, and was in the habit of swigging it for occasional distress. After a rich dinner and a number of drinks he had felt the need.

"Something was in it," said Nick.

"The doctor told me what it was," Ophelia said. "I can't remember. They're making a report out for the police."

"But they're letting him go home."

"Certainly," said Ophelia. She seemed surprised. "Why not? They know where to find him, after all. And they're keeping the Porcinox bottle."

Magaracz stood up, put his coat on, grabbed his wife and began to edge toward the exit. He was having second and third thoughts about taking this case. He said, "Well, okay, then, if there's nothing else, I guess we'll just . . ."

"Nick," Hester said, "We're counting on you now. Find the lunatic who's doing this to Howard and stop him."

"Sure," said Magaracz. "Sure, Hetty."

"I'll talk to the orchestra," the old lady said, "and offer to pay their cleaning bills."

The next morning Nick Magaracz got in the old T-bird and went back to Porcpharm. By the side of the road as he drove along he counted three deer carcasses, two raccoons, a squirrel, and a mangled house cat. The body count was up from yesterday by two deer. Other than that it was a nice day for a drive.

When he got to the office he went straight for the free coffee. He found a line of other employees in the little kitchen around the corner waiting to fill up their mugs, and joining the end of the line he passed the time by perusing the overflowing bulletin board.

There was a story cut from some trade magazine about the possibility of a merger between Porcineau Pharmaceuticals and Supraordinate Laboratories, headlined, "Porcpharm to be Swallowed like a Pill?" Supra Labs, it said here, was the largest drug conglomerate in the state of New Jersey, possibly the largest in the whole world. Certain paragraphs in the article had been marked in yellow highlighter and several discouraging words were scrawled at the end by an anonymous hand. So much for Howard's plan to keep the merger under wraps.

Business cards were tacked all over the bulletin board with pushpins, for nursing services, accounting services, lawn services, cordwood. The name of Kevin Mandelbaum leaped off the page of a brochure for company-provided social services. Magaracz remembered Mandelbaum as the sometime escort of Monica Nash, that woman who had wanted to dump her husband in a big tub of Drāno. Mandelbaum had an office here, according to the brochure, quite nearby if the room numbers weren't too badly out of line. You were supposed to give him a call if you suffered from family problems, drug or alcohol problems, unbearable financial pressure, or confusion. Somehow he would help you keep from screwing up on the job.

A notice of the monthly meeting of COGPAR, the Citizens of Greater Princeton for Animal Rights, with a woman's name and a phone number. Many phone numbers dangled from a notice of a motorcycle for sale; the numbers had been written sideways at the bottom of the notice, and snipped with scissors, forming a sort of fringe. A few had been torn off.

So crammed with solicitations and announcements was the bulletin board that the latest notices had to be tacked to the wall over the coffee machine. Most of these seemed to be memos from Howard Strass, regretfully announcing the allegedly voluntary resignation of this or that executive, and urging fellow employees to wish the ex-employee well in his or her future endeavors.

People getting coffee paused to read the very newest resignation memo, grunting in surprise or dismay before taking their coffee out of the kitchen in solemn silence. The man in front of Magaracz read the memo, uttered a particularly anguished groan, and drained the coffee pot, so that Magaracz got none.

He put up a fresh pot and retired to his office to meditate on his case while it brewed. Suppose that Howard's Porcinox had been doctored by somebody at Porcpharm. One possible way to get a handle on that would be to check everybody out, first of all by calling his brother-in-law at the Trenton police station. The lieutenant was in, and receiving calls, grudgingly.

"I'm up to my ass in paperwork, Nick," said Fennuccio. "What's up?"

"I need a favor," said Magaracz. "Run a check on these people for me." He gave a list of the principal suspects, including, just for the hell of it, all Howard's relatives.

"Sure," Fennuch said sourly. "I got nothing else to do."

"I owe you a beer, Fennuch," said Nick.

"You owe me a case of beer," the lieutenant replied. "I'll get back to you."

Magaracz put down his phone and gazed idly out the window as Howie Strass's Mercedes-Benz came rolling into the reserved parking spot with the sign saying HOWARD STRASS, PRESIDENT. The CEO got out and bounced up the steps to the main entrance as full of beans as if nothing had happened to him the night before.

A disquieting possibility occurred to Nick Magaracz: Howard had faked his own poisoning. How else to explain his blooming health, his obvious good humor, or the fact that the people in his own chemistry lab could find nothing harmful in the "poisonous" substances he brought them to test?

What if the whole poisoning scare was a figment of Howard Strass's sick mind? Magaracz was going to look like a jerk and a weenie for taking the job in the first place. *There goes my reputation in industrial espionage.* Geez, he might have to go back to work for the state. Unless there was some way to save the situation.

He could expose Howard Strass as a nut. But since Howard was the one who had hired him, it might discourage future clientele. Not discreet.

He could privately persuade Howard to drop his inquiry. That might be the way to go. Or, he could make Howard think that the poisoner—some mythical person—had somehow gone to a just reward, preferably due to Magaracz's efforts. That would cause Howard to pay him his fee and write a good recommendation.

But no. Why be false? Here he was again, working under the old bureaucratic maxim of cover your ass. What good was quitting the state if he couldn't get away from that stuff?

Also it might be that someone was really trying to kill Howard. Here was an idea: He would go to Howard's office and engage him in conversation, see what his attitude might be. The time had come for a little gentle, discreet probing.

Mary Mavis, Howard's secretary, wouldn't let him go into the boss's office. "He's in a meeting right now," she said. "You can wait if you want to. They're almost finished." She gestured toward a chair, and he sat in it. There were magazines on a table. He picked one up and pretended to read.

He could almost hear what was going on in the meeting, voices, and the tone of them, but not the words. A calm, confident baritone was speaking, measuring out sentences and paragraphs as though reading from a prepared speech. The baritone stopped speaking. After a short pause five or six other voices expressed unhappiness, all together and then one by one. Howard, interrupting, mumbled a little. Then they all came out of the office except for Howard.

The first man out of Howard's office was Magaracz's bet for the owner of the confident voice. Erect, alert, barrel chested, his hair as black as the raven in the parking lot, the man trod carelessly across the Chinese rug without a glance at Magaracz or Howard's secretary. He smelled of sandalwood and money. In his steady fist he gripped a fat leather briefcase of gleaming cordovan, and in his gabardine lapel he wore a tiny gold pin, whose shape Magaracz recognized as the capsule and beaker logo of Supraordinate Laboratories. *He's here to buy out the company,* Magaracz thought.

Then a handful of men and women in business suits followed, including Doctors Margaret Gagne and Carl Gables with his scarred face and his cast. Not one of those who emerged wore the assurance of the first guy; not one paid any attention to Mary Mavis, or seemed to notice Nick Magaracz. All, in fact, appeared to be suffering varying degrees of gastric distress. Actors auditioning for a cure-all commercial. "This is vice president Smith before taking Porcinox." Must have been quite a meeting.

Mrs. Mavis put her head in the boss's door and murmured something. He murmured back. "You can go in now," she said to Magaracz.

He found the chief executive loading up the Mr. Coffee machine in his inner office. A faint odor persisted, of sandalwood and flop sweat.

"Howard," the detective said to Howard's back. "How's it going?"

"Fine," said Howard. "What can I do for you this morning, Nick?"

"Howard, I need to know why somebody would want to poison you."

Howard Strass did one last thing to the coffee machine and turned to face him, massaging his scalp, rubbing away the thoughts of the meeting, maybe, and redirecting his attention to the matter at hand.

"I haven't the remotest idea, Nick," he said, sitting down in the brown leather chair behind his desk. "It's a complete mystery. That's why you were hired, you know." He began to play with some wrapped toffees in a lacquered bowl.

"But maybe after last night people will believe me," he went on. "It's depressing when something like this is happening to be told it's all in your mind." He stared at his hands, playing with the candies. For a long time the only sound was the burbling of Mr. Coffee.

Then Howard took the two ends of the toffee wrapping between his thumbs and forefingers and pulled. The toffee twirled around three times and fell out of its wrapping onto the desk blotter.

"Why would someone want to poison me? I don't know," he said. "Why doesn't the lab ever find anything in the things I send them? I don't know that either," he said, popping the toffee in his mouth. "Maybe somebody in the lab is tampering with the evidence." Suddenly with a startled expression he spit the toffee into his hand, looked at it, and put it in the ashtray.

This guy is crazy, said Magaracz to himself. But, okay, he would try out the tampering theory. "What about this Burton Pollert?" he said. "He works in the lab. What is he to you?"

"Nothing," said Strass, pulling a white handkerchief from his breast pocket and wiping his hand on it. "An employee. Is Burton Pollert the one?"

"You tell me, Howie."

"If he is, it must be because he's mentally ill. He certainly has no logical reason to try to kill me," said Strass, smoothing his hairs. "Maybe he's attacking the company through me, as I suggested to you before."

"Okay, then, in another vein, what can you tell me about Carl Gables's injuries?"

The hands stopped rubbing the bald spot. "What do you mean?"

"How did he break the arm? What happened to his face? Tell me."

"Why don't you ask him?"

"I'm asking you, Howard."

"I haven't any way of knowing. Didn't he walk into a door?"

"Hell of a door," said Magaracz. A random thought wandered into his mind, and sprang to his lips before he could censor it: "What was he, on dope?"

The chief executive stood up, angry. "Carl Gables is my wife's brother-in-law," he said. "He couldn't possibly have anything to do with trying to poison me. This is getting us nowhere. Tell me something. Do you want to continue with this case?"

"Oh, sure, if I have anything to work with," said Magaracz.

"Then get out there and find something to work with."

The coffee maker had stopped making noises. It smelled pretty good. "Mind if I have a cup of coffee first?" said Magaracz.

"Go right ahead," said Howard. There were plastic cups by the coffee maker, plastic stirrers, artificial sugar, powdered non-dairy cream substitute.

It was the worst coffee he had ever tasted.

Seven

The privileged few vice presidents and department heads who had been given advance notice of the merger had strict instructions neither to tell their subordinates nor to call their brokers. The public announcement was scheduled to be made at noon in Hackensack by the management of Supraordinate Laboratories, the drug giant which would henceforth refer to itself as the parent company, although it had nothing to do with Porcpharm's conception, gestation, or early nurturance. At the same time a general meeting was to be called in Princeton to tell the Porcpharm rank and file. So those who were in on the secret had to keep it for only an hour.

Two of the vice presidents went straight from the

meeting in Howard's office to the Fox, where they proceeded to drink their faces off.

Dr. Margaret Gagne returned to her own office overlooking the chem lab and began to list and evaluate her subordinates.

Howard Strass called home to crow to his wife about the excellent price he was able to get for her Porcpharm shares. But the maid said she was out. It was all the same, he realized. Ophelia was strangely indifferent to money, possibly because she had always had it. Nevertheless, he told himself, whether she was aware of it or not this merger would make an enormous difference in their lives.

Dr. Carl Gables did not rush out and practice substance abuse, nor yet did he sit down and critically analyze his blissfully unknowing staff, since he was well aware that when Supra Labs moved in and took over their competence would no more be an issue than would his own. He did call his wife. She ought to be told what was going on; after all, it was, or had been, her family's business.

"The merger has gone through, then," she said.

He said, "Yes, Howard has sold the business and now it will be a wholly owned subsidiary of Supraordinate Laboratories."

"What happens now?" she said.

"We'll have to see," said Gables. "I think there'll be some big changes. But we'll have to see what happens." They said good-bye, and he hung up the phone and contemplated his tidy bulletin board with its carefully worked out schedules. Maybe the events on those schedules would come to pass, and maybe not. Suddenly he thought of several things that he might never get a chance to do again; he got up and did them.

*   *   *

When at the age of nineteen Caroline Porcineau had first met Carl Gables, she had found it enormously exciting to consort with a man so completely repugnant to her family. Carl was hairy, and his fingernails were dirty, and he said "youse" and "beau-dee-ful," and as for his table manners, they were so bad as to cause even her father to turn pale and clear his throat. So she married him. To her annoyance the family thereupon proceeded to clasp him to its bosom, send him through school, buy them a house, and set him up with a job at Porcineau Pharmaceuticals.

With the end of her adolescence, what her family thought of him mattered less and less to her. Their third child was born, her father died (and not of outrage at her marrying Carl), the bloom was off their physical passion. He was no longer her knight of the proletariat; he was just Carl. Over the years he had grown both more socially acceptable and more distant. He didn't say "youse" any more. If he called any woman "beau-dee-ful," it wasn't her. Perhaps his table manners had improved; she never saw him at mealtime.

One day she became convinced that there was another woman in his life. He was home very seldom, to begin with, and paid no attention to her when he was home. It was inconceivable to Caroline that a man with Carl's insistent physical needs should have no outlet for them at all. Of course there was another woman.

She knew that Howard had a mistress; Ophelia had confided in her one tearful afternoon. Why not Carl, then? If that was what men were all about. But she was unable to be as modern and European about his supposed infidelity as she had hoped to be. Although she had convinced herself that she no longer cared for Carl, the idea of his having anyone else made her terribly sad. She wept for an entire afternoon, precipitating a three-day migraine.

But time went on and she was able to convince herself that she had been mistaken. A little detective work, checking the odometer on his car, perusing the telephone bills, suggested that there was nothing in Carl's life more interesting than his work, which absorbed him completely. A workaholic. She could live with that.

Men weren't everything. There was always food. Food, the children, the Great Books group . . . really, she led a very full and interesting life.

Still the specter of the Other Woman lurked in the back of her mind to pounce at times when she was feeling low and insecure, just before her period, for instance, or when one of the children messed up at school. Then the Woman would appear, strutting, boobies jiggling, her skirt slashed to the waist, and laugh her nasty little laugh of triumph.

What Caroline did when one of these mental attacks came on was to go over the concrete things again, the contents of all his pockets, the function of all his keys, her secret odometer diary, the phone bill, Carl's American Express bills (which she always steamed open when they came), and the checks returned by the bank. To account for all the miles and the money seemed to her the same as accounting for all of Carl's erotic energy.

Days when the long distance phone bills came were the worst.

Just enough information appeared on these bills to

fuel Caroline's panic attacks. Who in the household would have placed an evening call to such-and-such a number in Rocky Hill? Visions came unbidden of Carl, whispering a few late-night words to the negligee-clad popsie as she lounged in their Rocky Hill love nest, before slinking between the passionless sheets with his wife. Upon investigation, the dreaded phone number would prove to be that of the cook's aged mother. Caroline tracked it down by dialing the number and, when someone answered, pretending to be taking a survey. Suddenly she would remember: *Ah, this is Mrs. Rajametik's mother.* Relief! Carl was innocent. But what about this next mysterious charge? And so forth. One untoward by-product of her investigative method was the list of mysterious numbers, called by herself and then forgotten, that confronted Caroline on the following month's bill.

Oh, yes. She knew it was sick. But she couldn't help herself.

But when the actual blow came she was not looking for it, or expecting it. She was simply using Carl's checkbook to write a check to pay the maid. The previous entry leaped out at her: $38,000 to di Orio Motors.

What could this be? At once the image formed in Caroline's mind of The Woman, blond, slim, dressed and perfumed like the expensive floozie she was, cruising the roads of Central Jersey in a sleek $38,000 convertible paid for in cash by her Carl. Foiling the careful odometer diary. They could go anywhere now! The mileage would never show.

But wait. Stop. If Carl were seeing someone else, where were the other clues, the bills for motels and restaurants, the strange telephone numbers on the long distance bill, the stains on his laundry?

Anyway her birthday was next week. Of course. What could she have been thinking of? Carl was giving her a car for her birthday. Last year he had forgotten her birthday altogether. Probably he was going to make it up to her this year. Of course he still loved her. Hadn't he called her from work, that very morning? Still the picture of the blond lingered, waving from the driver's seat of the convertible, smiling with perfect teeth, her mouth a red slash.

Magaracz found his new office after a couple of wrong turns, and there he sat down and considered his position. Not vis-à-vis the merger; he cared nothing about that, but rather with regard to his career in industrial espionage in general, and this case in particular.

He could find out who was against the merger. He could find out who the girlfriend was. That shouldn't be too hard, particularly in an affair of long standing; just plug into the rumor mill. He could shadow Buddy Pollert. He could find out who beat up Carl Gables, when, and why.

Outside his window, the raven had come back; he could see it pecking, pecking at something in the grass. All this thinking was giving him a headache. The air in the building was bad; the office was poorly ventilated; in an attempt to clear his lungs, Magaracz went out to take a walk on the grounds.

This must be the old man's golf course, he thought. Rumor had it that Howard Strass's father-in-law, an avid golfer, had a nine hole course installed out on the grounds somewhere, where he had played a round or two in the afternoons before his heart attack had sent him to the big country club in the sky. Nobody had played here lately. The greens keeper must have been let go as an economy measure; the grass was knee-high, and little evergreen trees were springing up all over.

There was a sand trap, a sunny, pleasant-looking place, and there Magaracz decided to sit for a minute until this dizziness went away. But as he approached it he noticed a bad smell.

Garbage, he said to himself. People dumped their garbage in the damnedest places. As he looked around, though, he didn't see anything that could be garbage, and as he looked more closely at the sand-bank he realized it didn't look normal.

There were holes in the bank, little black holes smaller than a dime, and something was moving . . . Big grains of sand, or something sand-colored, streaming from the holes, running down the bank into a puddle . . . moving . . . writhing . . .

Maggots.

Streams of little maggots were issuing from fissures in the sandbank, falling down and pooling at the bottom.

Magaracz turned and headed back toward the main building. It wasn't easy getting there, because the whole lawn had started to heave and roll like the surface of the ocean. His ears were ringing. His head was killing him. It was hard to put his feet down without falling. Still, it was important to get back so he could find the people responsible for maintaining the building and grounds and tell them about the maggots. Besides, he really needed something to drink.

He got onto the pavement, finally. The concrete was

kind of rough. He hoped it wouldn't put holes in the knees of his good suit. No telling what Ethel would say. He was almost at the door. He reached out for it. Only, the front of the building was moving, slipping past, and slipping past, and slipping . . .

Eight

A half-empty pack of Pall Malls lay beside the overflowing ashtray on Margaret Gagne's desk. Arthur Munsen, waiting for her to come out of the laboratory and see him, took one and lit it. He was trying to quit smoking and so not carrying any of his own brand. But this was a stressful moment. He had come to put the hurt on his old lover to pressure her for her favors.

His pulses were pounding. Blackmailing people always caused him the most unbearable excitement.

He hadn't smoked an unfiltered cigarette in years; after all this time, they tasted funny.

A little fellow with greasy yellow hair and pockmarks came out of the lab. "Are you waiting to see Dr. Gagne?" he asked.

"Yes. Could you remind her?"

"I'm sorry," he said, "but she's gone out the other way. There's a meeting of all the employees in the atrium at noon. I'm going there myself." He went out past the guard and down the hall before Munsen could ask him anything about the meeting. Maybe he should have read his electronic mail today.

He took one last drag on the foul-tasting cigarette, ground it out, and went to join the other employees in the atrium.

The electronic mail message that Munsen had missed had been posted since eleven-thirty:

THERE WILL BE A MEETING IN THE ATRIUM TODAY AT TWELVE O'CLOCK NOON. ALL EMPLOYEES ARE URGED TO ATTEND. AN IMPORTANT ANNOUNCEMENT WILL BE MADE CONCERNING THE FUTURE OF THIS COMPANY.

Stories flew around the rumor mill. One was that Big Howie Strass had sold Porcineau Pharmaceuticals. No one could agree on who the buyer was. Another story had Howie poisoned to death. That one was being circulated by someone who had seen a man put into an ambulance and taken away by the Hillsboro Rescue Squad. This was disputed by another person, who had seen the victim's face. It wasn't Howie. It might have been the detective who was here.

They were certain of only one thing: Half of them were about to be fired.

Margaret Gagne, serene in her inside knowledge, held herself aloof from the speculations of her fellow workers as she made her way to the atrium to hear Howard announce the big news. It never occurred to her that hers could be among the heads when they rolled.

Was she not the developer of the drug that was

destined to significantly slow the spread of AIDS? A biochemist with her credentials could get work anywhere in the world. Porcpharm would never let her go, never, and neither would anyone who bought them out, and even if they did there were better jobs out there.

What would most likely happen was that the man from Supra Labs would fire everybody who could help her get her work done and she would be stuck here with maybe three other chemists and one lab technician for the three of them. And probably he would also cancel Porcpharm's plans to buy the Fourier transform mass spectrometer she had requested.

Well, that was the system for you. Maybe it was time to move on. The good news was that this would be the perfect chance to lay her ax to some of the deadwood, the goof-offs, the druggies, the persons who for whatever reason were less than diligent in the performance of their duties.

Buddy Pollert, for instance.

And here was another idea. Maybe Howard himself, now that he had sold the company, would go away and she would no longer be troubled with the sight of his pasty face with its ever-growing jowls. When he was young he had been a lot of fun. But that was then.

In those days Margaret Gagne still retained that quality that had made her so successful as a stripper, working her way through graduate school, the quality of reflecting back the fantasies that men projected onto her. As time went on the effort of playacting became too bothersome and her own sour character asserted itself. But Howard had been able to see her as some sort of heavy earth mother—it must have been her hips—and he nursed a desire to get a son on her, something he could never manage with Ophelia. He seemed to feel it would validate his manhood. She never told him she was on the pill; no point in it.

He was kind of sweet actually. For several months she had been passionately in love with him, safe enough since he was so firmly married. Then one day she noticed a vertical wrinkle that seemed to have formed in front of his left ear. It completely changed the aspect of his face. At that moment—they were making love at the time—whatever she had felt for him evaporated completely. Slowly by degrees she eased him out of her life.

In the cavernous atrium the employees were beginning to collect, some hanging over the balcony rails, some on the stairs, others gathering at the foot of the podium in anticipation of Howard Strass's appearance. *Ah, Howard, can it be that I'll finally see the last of you?* Then she had to ask herself whether that was what she really and truly wanted. No, what she truly wanted was a cigarette and a tumbler full of bourbon. The cigarette would have to do.

Buddy appeared. "Did that man ever find you?" he asked.

"Man—? Oh, him. No." No matches. "Buddy, have you got a light?"

"Sure, Dr. G," he said, searching his pockets. "He seemed quite anxious to talk to you."

"The anxiety was all on his side," Margaret replied. Carl Gables came gimping up. The wound on his head was bright red.

"I'm sure you know that this is a nonsmoking area now," he said, as Buddy Pollert held a match to her cigarette. Buddy started in a guilty fashion, causing her cigarette to fail to light.

"For crissake, Buddy," she said, "give me the goddam matches." Next he would be setting her nose on fire.

Buddy relinquished the matches, then glanced at Gables as though expecting to be hit. *Stop groveling,* she wanted to say to him. It must be tough to have two bosses. That was another thing that would have to change under the new order, this business of braiding the organization chart, today I report to you, tomorrow to him, but a third person does my performance review. She hoped that Jared Baines would be reasonable about these matters. She also hoped he would be reasonable about the spectrometer.

"But don't let it stop you," said Gables. He gave her a strange look, staring into her eyes, almost smiling. Like Buddy, he was breathing through his mouth.

"What?" she said.

"Don't let it stop you, the fact that this area is no-smoking."

"Okay," she said. She blew a long stream of cigarette smoke out of her nose at him. "So how about it, Carl? Got your résumé together?" she said.

"There's plenty of time," he said. He had black hair growing out of his nostrils. Ugh. Come to think of it, Carl had black hair all over.

Carl could easily lose his job now, if the Porcineaus gave up their interest in the company entirely. He would no longer have the protection of his wife's family.

"Ah, here's Howard," said Carl, making a place for Margaret at the balcony rail. "Now he'll explain everything." He pressed right up next to her; she had to move away from him to break contact, bumping into Buddy. It was too crowded here. She thought of finding a better spot, but this was the best view of the podium, and sure enough, here was Howard.

The CEO stepped up to the microphone, and tapped on it, and the public address system gave out with an excruciating whine. At length it stopped, and he spoke.

"Fellow employees."

Respectful attention.

"As most of you know, this has been a difficult year for Porcineau Pharmaceuticals. Due to a thirty percent shortfall in revenues, we have been forced to freeze hiring, minimize discretionary spending, consolidate positions, and terminate personnel where performance was marginal. Nevertheless we are in a very competitive position in a high-growth, exciting industry and we are confident that the success that Porcineau Pharmaceuticals has enjoyed in the past will continue in the future." Margaret yawned into her hand, discreetly.

"I wish to announce that we have had an offer to merge with Supraordinate Laboratories. Their offer has been accepted."

For a moment the afternoon sun pouring through the skylight was blocked, as if by a black cloud or a flock of turkey buzzards. A shiver went through the crowd, a shuddering indrawing of breath that seemed to include the philodendrons and Benjamin fig trees, as if even they could sense the coming of the pruning shears.

"We feel that the support and backing of such an industry giant as Supra Labs can only strengthen our competitive position in the drug industry," Howard continued, as though oblivious to the sensation he was creating. "We look forward to your continuing efforts

on behalf of Porcineau Pharmaceuticals to keep us
among the leaders in the field.

"At this time I would like to introduce Mr. Jared
Baines of Supraordinate Laboratories."

Stern in a black suit, the man from Supra Labs
might have been made of granite as he stepped up to
address the troops. He gave the usual speech, praising
them for their dedication in the past, urging them to
even greater efforts in the future. Then he invited
questions from the floor.

Embarrassed silence.

Then the green plants themselves seemed to writhe
as a voice called out, "Is it true, sir, that the staff will
be cut by five hundred?"

The man from Supra Labs stared with hard eyes. "I
will hide nothing from you," he said at last. "There will
be no duplication of functions. We have discussed this
problem at considerable length and we have made a
determination that Porcineau Pharmaceuticals is over-
staffed by perhaps three hundred. But certainly not
five hundred. There is no reason to panic."

In spite of his words, a wave of panic spread over the
assembled crowd like wind across a wheat field.

"Most of these people will be lost through attrition
and simply not replaced," Baines continued. "Of
course, there are entire departments here performing
the same functions as those already in place at Supraordinate Laboratories. In these cases, we feel it
may . . ."

Suddenly there was a high-pitched scream from the
upper balcony. A body plummeted to the tiles at Jared
Baines's feet.

Howard Strass stepped down from the dais and knelt
beside the crumpled form. He seemed to be sniffing,

for bitter almonds, no doubt; then he felt for a pulse and looked up.

"Dead," he said. The victim was none other than poor Artie Munsen. Everyone knew that Supraordinate Laboratories had their own public relations department.

"That's one," someone whispered.

Nine

![black bar]

A swarthy East Indian stood over Magaracz when he opened his eyes, with glossy black hair, dressed all in white and wearing a stethoscope around his neck. "I'm Dr. Dey," he said. "How are you feeling?"

"Terrible," said Nick. "That was the worst cup of coffee I ever drank." It was hard for him to talk; there seemed to be something in his mouth. He realized it was his tongue.

"Your wife is outside. I'll send her in to you."

"So what was in the coffee?" he said to the doctor.

"Diphenhydramine hydrochloride," the doctor said. "Over-the-counter cold medicine. Maybe other drugs as well, but that was what had been in the empty containers they found by the coffee machine."

"Can that stuff kill you?"

"It has been known to cause respiratory failure."

"I'm breathing okay. Can I go home now?" From the needle sticking in his arm, Magaracz figured the answer would be no, but it couldn't hurt to try.

"We want to keep you here for another day or two," Dr. Dey said. "You aren't quite out of danger yet. Some patients experience central nervous system stimulation from antihistamine drugs and we want to wait for your gastric and cardiovascular functions to return to normal. I'll send your wife in now."

Magaracz didn't think to ask what central nervous system stimulation might be. He didn't feel stimulated; he didn't even feel like getting up, even if there hadn't been an IV stuck in his arm. Maybe it was mental.

Mental . . . like the maggots in the golf course. But no, that was real. There was a body buried out there.

Ethel came in and gave him a hug and a kiss. "Well, Nick," she said, "are you ready to go back to work for the state?"

"Gimme a break," he said. There was a huge flower arrangement on his windowsill. He said, "What's that? I ain't seen nothing like that since your Uncle Louie cashed."

"Ophelia Strass sent them. Wasn't that nice?"

"No," he said. "I hate flowers."

"They say you might be in here awhile. Are you okay?" she said.

"I've been better, but sure, I'm okay."

"You look awful."

"What time of day is it?"

"Five-thirty in the afternoon. You've been here since yesterday, hon," she said.

"Gimme the phone, will you? I've got to report a

dead body." She handed the phone to him and then stared in wonderment as he dialed 911.

"Hi, I want to report an occurrence of maggots. . . . a whole lot of suspicious maggots on the golf course at Porcineau Pharmaceuticals."

That wasn't exactly what he had wanted to say, but before he could rephrase his message a nurse came in with a tray full of medicines and hypodermic needles. He saw her at first out of the corner of his eye, and what she appeared to be was a large fish, a bluefish maybe, with scaly legs, dressed in a nurse's uniform. This was so unusual that it caused him to drop the phone and shout.

When he looked straight at her she turned back into a regular nurse again. Maybe this was what the doctor meant by central nervous system stimulation. Ethel took the phone away from him and said something about how he needed his rest. The bluefish stuck another needle in him.

He sank into a terrifying and interminable dream. Everyone from Porcpharm was in it, and all Howard's relatives. Dr. Carl Gables took him and put him in a cage, and put an iron collar and a chain around his neck. Magaracz kept telling everyone that he didn't really work there. He worked for the State of New Jersey. They had to let him go. But no, they said he was a lab animal and they were going to do experiments on him. Ophelia tried to make him eat flowers, and Hester endeavored to get him to take Wankemol capsules and wash them down with glasses of coffee and blood.

Then monkeys came and tore his clothes off, and forced him to attend the performance of an opera, stark naked, at the War Memorial building; Buddy Pollert and Margaret Gagne were the stars. They bellowed off-key love songs at one another until all the monkeys threw things at them. Then the monkeys took Nick by the heels and hung him over the balcony and dropped him, and he fell down into a bottomless pit that grew blacker and blacker. Many other things happened in his dream, terrible things, but when he woke he forgot everything but the opera and the monkeys, and falling.

It was the middle of the night.

He couldn't get back to sleep.

When he was home and not sleeping, he could always get up and watch television, or at least turn on the light and read. But the nurses here wouldn't let him do that, and he was forced to endure a long night of sleeplessness with no other entertainment than to put his bed up and down, or watch the nurses wiggling in and out of his room, wearing the shapes of various animals. The bluefish was off duty then, but the night nurse was a hulking ape with enormous yellow fangs. The ape's uniform was too tight, and tufts of hair stuck out in front between the button closings. For some reason she kept trying to get him to pee in a cup.

"I have to measure your output," she insisted. "That's the rule when you have an IV. If you won't go in the container, you know, we're going to have to catheterize you."

"You'll have to catch me first, sister," he said, retreating to the far corner of the bed. The ape nurse sighed with annoyance, and stamped her foot.

"The day nurses will know how to deal with you," she said ominously, and left. He dragged his IV unit to the bathroom and peed in the toilet like a normal person, perhaps for the last time. Catheterize him. Why had Ophelia Strass sent him flowers? Was she being nice? Or was she feeling guilty because he got the poison that was meant for Howard?

She knew about the girlfriend. The wife always does. She poisoned Howard's coffee at work to divert suspicion. Maybe Buddy Pollert was in it with her. There was nothing to write with—they had taken away his notebook—and so Magaracz was forced to let his theories drift away with the night's bad dreams.

In the morning he was saved from a fate worse than death by the arrival of the day nurse, who by a happy coincidence was none other than Uncle Louie's eldest daughter.

"Concetta!" he said. "Thank God it's you." She even looked like herself, not like an animal or anything.

"Hi, Nick," she said. "Sorry you got poisoned. How do you feel?" She plumped up his pillow, and took his pulse, and did nurse things.

"Pretty good," he said. "Say, how do you like those flowers?"

"All right," she said. "Reminds me of Dad's funeral, though."

"Didn't one of his friends send flowers just like that?"

"Right," she said. "Asters and lemon leaves, with white carnations. Uncle Chickie called up and sent it from Ossining. They wouldn't let him out to come to the funeral. Hey, Nick, Bernice tells me you've been a very bad boy."

"She the night nurse?"

"Right. You know, you have to pee in the cup. We're supposed to measure it."

"Bureaucrats, everywhere you go," he said. But it was good to have a friend there. Then it struck him:

Concetta was a nurse. She had access to hospital records. "Hey, listen," he said. "Could you look something up for me?"

"Like what?" she said.

"I was hoping they would have a record here of a man who was admitted to this hospital through the emergency room with—oh, I don't know—multiple trauma or something. His name is Carl Gables. I want to know exactly what was wrong with him."

"If I can find that out for you, will you pee in the cup for me?"

"Yes."

"I'll be back in half an hour. Don't urinate in the toilet."

"I promise."

After she left they brought him breakfast: rubber eggs and some very uninteresting toast. He couldn't face the sight of the coffee, any coffee, and turned the saucer upside down on top of the cup. Tomorrow's menu came with his meal. Tomorrow? Would he be here tomorrow? And was this what they would expect him to eat? While he was trying to choose from among the available foods they moved a guy into the other bed.

Evidently the guy came straight from the recovery room, where he had been recuperating from the effects of an operation of some kind on his foot. It was puffy with bandages. Thin, pale, and shaky, the roommate offered Magaracz a wan smile, barely visible behind his bushy salt-and-pepper moustache and beard. There was something goatlike about his appearance. "I'm Jonathan Fine," he said. "I shot myself in the foot. What are you in for?"

"Nick Magaracz," he replied. "I was poisoned."

"Wow," said the roommate. "How did that happen?"

"It's a mystery to me," said Magaracz. "I'm a detective. What were you, cleaning your gun?"

"Didn't shoot myself with a gun. Shot myself with a bow and arrow."

"Sounds hard to do," said Magaracz. As he watched, Jonathan Fine began to turn strangely gray and furry.

"Do you know anything about Zen archery?" said Fine.

"No," said Magaracz.

"Well, I guess I know less about it than I needed to. Anyway it has to do with letting the arrow shoot itself."

"So it shot itself into your foot," said Magaracz.

"Pretty much," said Fine.

They lay in silence for awhile, Fine no doubt engaging in Zen meditations and Magaracz waiting for the undulations of the room to subside. Central nervous system stimulation seemed to be something that came and went. At last the walls stopped spinning. Fine turned and smiled at him with pink goat lips, crinkling the corners of his strange golden eyes, whose pupils appeared to be vertical slits.

Ten

W hen Magaracz awoke from his nap, Jonathan
Fine had somehow struggled to his hind hooves and
was performing calisthenics.

Concetta came in. "What are you doing!" she cried.

Fine replied, "The Yogi's salute to the sun."

"You can't do that," she said. "You can't do anything like that. Not for six weeks. Get back in bed."

"Better do as she says," said Magaracz. "She's
pretty tough."

Fine got back in bed. Concetta took his pulse and
said, "Tsk."

Then she pulled the curtain all around Magaracz and
revealed to him in hushed tones what she had found
out from the hospital records. It was this: Carl Gables

had been brought in stark naked, suffering from multiple contusions and a broken wrist.

"The chart said that his injuries were inconsistent with his story of having run into a door."

"What were they consistent with?"

"It says here, 'Physician suggests that he was beaten with a broom handle or some such implement.' He was in for a week, by the way."

"Some door," said Magaracz. "No wonder there's a guard on it."

"Right," she said. "Now pee in the cup, please."

For as long as he could remember, Carl Gables had loved animals. He admired their spirits, their souls, and their little warm furry bodies as well. When he was growing up his dog meant more to him than any other member of his family, because she was more loyal, never criticized him, and slept with him every night.

No human could compete with that.

It was no mere coincidence that the woman he married had the same name as his long-dead dog, the first true love of his life.

Caroline Porcineau was the daughter of a family of considerable wealth. She paid his way through veterinary college. He looked forward to setting up a practice treating household pets, lovable creatures, curing their ills and behavior problems and putting them gently to sleep when all else failed. But it was not to be. A condition of marrying into the Porcineau family was that you had to work for one of the family businesses.

Porcineau Pharmaceuticals needed a head veterinarian for their animal laboratories. The money was very good and it was strongly suggested to young Dr.

Gables that the Porcineaus expected a decent return on their investment in his career, the better to support their daughter. So he took the job. But as the years went by his position gnawed at him, corrupting him in subtle ways.

He had to hurt the animals, you see, or let them be hurt.

He thought, "I will save enough money to quit and go into business for myself." But Caroline and the children spent everything and more. He couldn't get any purchase on the project. And then, to complicate his troubles—or, perhaps, to simplify them—he fell in love.

He was meditating on these events as Jared Baines, the hatchet man from Supra Labs, appeared in the monkey laboratory without announcing himself. The guard had some dim idea that Baines was the new boss and buzzed him right in.

"I've come to measure the room," he said to the veterinarian. "Please don't let me disturb you. Go right ahead with whatever it is you're doing."

"You don't disturb me, Baines," said Gibbons, "but you might be disturbing the animals. Tell me, why weren't you announced before they let you in here?"

"Oh, I wouldn't worry very much about the animals, if I were you," said Baines. "Hold this end, will you?" He gave the end of the tape to Gables, and paid it out until it reached halfway to the opposite wall. "Supra Labs has plenty of animals." He made a mark on the floor. "Thank you. Now hold the end right here, while I . . ."

"Surely you realize that these aren't just animals, this is a research laboratory. Most of these creatures are being used right now to test new products for

Porcineau Pharmaceuticals and those that aren't are serving as controls."

"Right there," said Baines. "Hold it steady. But surely *you* must realize, Dr. Gables, that between the high cost of product testing and development and the high cost of litigation, new drugs are simply not cost-effective. Supra Labs is not in business for its health. Thank you." He reeled in the steel measuring tape and wrote some numbers in a notebook. "Then, of course," he added, "many of the functions that were once performed by animal testing can now be handled by electronic equipment, which Supraordinate Laboratories already has in abundance. No duplication of functions. We announced that, you will recall." He closed the book and put the tape in his pocket.

"What will happen to these animals?" said Gables.

"Oh, probably they'll be destroyed. Certainly the infected ones will. The clean animals," he said, "some of the ones you've been using as controls, might be sold or donated to a zoo. That would be good for the company's image. Don't you agree?"

It wasn't until the man had left that Gables thought to wonder why he hadn't sent his flunkies to measure the lab. Apparently he was indulging in a ritual display of male dominance. *Here's mine, they're brass.* Gables had not been out-and-about enough in corporate culture to understand what the appropriate counter-display should have been, the here's-mine-they're-iron move. Even thinking about it afterwards, he couldn't think of anything he could have done to save his face, his laboratory, his way of life, or himself from Jared Baines. Except perhaps to kill him. And there were plenty more where he came from.

No, there was nothing to do but tough it out and carry on with his original plan.

Ethel's brother Frank, the Trenton police lieutenant, called Nick Magaracz in the hospital around one o'clock in the afternoon. Magaracz wasn't exactly sleeping, but neither was he very wide awake.

"Nick," said Fennuccio. "Sorry to hear you got poisoned."

"Yeah. Right. Me too."

"So how you feeling?"

"I've been better, but I guess I'll live."

"Ethel told me you went crazy. You in your right mind yet?"

Aside from a few strange phenomena, such as the aquarium that someone seemed to have installed on the ceiling while he was napping, the room looked pretty normal. "Far as I can tell," Magaracz allowed.

"Ready to hear what I got for you?"

"Sure, Fennuch, ready as I'll ever be. Shoot."

"Everybody on the list you gave me is clean, as far as the police records are concerned. Except three."

"Namely?"

"Burton Pollert has been arrested twice for possession of a controlled dangerous substance," said Fennuccio.

"Figures."

"Howard Strass owes the City of Trenton seven hundred and fifty dollars in tickets for parking in front of his mother-in-law's house on West State Street."

"Also figures. Who's the third one?"

"Get this. Ophelia Porcineau Strass was busted in

Princeton for disturbing the peace and resisting arrest.''

"Antiwar protesting," Magaracz guessed.

"No. This was only three years ago. Antivivisectionist demonstrations. She got arrested for supporting
animal rights at Porcineau Pharmaceuticals.''

Magaracz thanked him profusely and asked to be
sent the particulars in writing.

"Aw, don't ask me to *write* nothing, Nick," begged
the lieutenant. "I already got six reports to do.''

"Well, can't you get them to stick the police report
in the fax machine?''

"Cost you ten bucks for a copy of the police report.''

"I owe you ten bucks," said Magaracz.

"And a case of Coors," Fennuccio reminded him.

"Right. A case of Coors.''

"See you," said Fennuccio. "Get well quick.''

Looking up, Magaracz was relieved to see that the
aquarium had gone away. His roommate, however, had
completely metamorphosed into a horned billy goat.
Raised up on one elbow, his bedclothes draped in a
simple fold across his slim brown hairy body, Jonathan
Fine regarded him from the other hospital bed with a
curious golden stare.

"You okay, man?" Fine inquired.

"Swell," said Magaracz. "Did you notice who took
those fish away?''

"You're hallucinating, aren't you?" the goat asked
gently.

"Me?" said Magaracz. "Hell, no. You guys are all
turning into things.''

"Such as what?" asked Fine.

"Fish. Monkeys. Goats." Magaracz was embarrassed. Maybe it wasn't real.

"Now, listen carefully," said Fine. "I'm a psychologist. I can help you. You are under the influence of drugs."

"Drugs. Right. Central nervous system stimulation," he mumbled.

"You're tripping. You're on another plane of existence."

Magaracz tried to make a crack about planes and airports, but he couldn't quite formulate it.

Fine said, "As long as you're doing this anyway, what you ought to do is take advantage of it for spiritual growth."

"What!?"

"Your subconscious mind is telling you things, bringing you insight into the characters of the people around you. Go with it," the goat advised. "Take notes. Write everything down. When you come down I'll give you my card. You can call me if you have any problems later."

His advice sounded logical and reassuring. Magaracz resolved to follow it, just as soon as he found some paper and pencil. As soon as he had a little nap and got rid of this headache.

Eleven

Magaracz awoke to find that visiting hours had come and Hester Porcineau was standing over him with a large bouquet. They were running out of room on the windowsill for all these flowers.

"Hiya, Hettie," he said.

"Nick, I'm sorry you got poisoned."

"How's Howard?" he asked, remembering for the first time that it was Howard's coffee that had poisoned him.

"Fine. He had a funny feeling about that coffee and never drank it. But, you know, Nick, he has funny feelings about everything."

"It's a wonder he isn't losing weight," said Magaracz.

"He is," she said.

Suddenly Magaracz thought of his hallucinations. Were they gone? Hester Porcineau looked normal. He glanced over at the other bed; Jonathan Fine wasn't there. Good. He could talk privately with Hester.

"Sit down, Hettie," he invited. "Take a load off."

"Why thank you, Nick. I believe I will." The old lady found a place for the flower arrangement and planted herself in the plastic chair provided for visitors.

"I need to talk to you," he said.

"I'm all ears."

"What's the story on Ophelia's rap sheet?" he asked.

"Nick," she said reproachfully.

"You were hoping I wouldn't turn up her police record."

"You weren't hired to investigate the family, Nick," she said. "We aren't trying to poison anyone."

"Tell me the story anyway," he said.

Hester Porcineau looked at him for a long moment, making up her mind whether to trust him or fire him, probably. She liked him, and she was a nice lady, but when it came to certain things she could be pretty tough. You had to be, to keep all that money. And if your money wouldn't protect your family, what good was it?

At last she sighed, and decided to open up. To a limited degree.

"Ophelia is very idealistic," said Hester Porcineau. "Most people of her generation are."

"Okay."

"She was never one of the hippies, but she was in Africa with the Peace Corps for two years. Since she came home she has always been involved with some bleeding-heart group or other.''

"So?" he said.

"She was manipulated by those COGPAR people into making a fool of herself. They used her, Nick, to embarrass the family.''

"COGPAR," he repeated. They posted notices on the office bulletin board.

"Citizens of Greater Princeton for Animal Rights. They got Ophelia to picket Porcineau Pharmaceuticals. Someone told them we were using live animal studies to develop drugs. They didn't know whether or not the animals were being maltreated. They just thought that if they could involve Ophelia it would make a good story for the papers.''

"I don't remember seeing anything in the press about it," said Magaracz.

"Come now, Nick," said the old lady. "I'm not completely without influence in this state.''

She had persuaded them to kill the story. "So did she quit doing that stuff when she figured out they were using her? Or did she ever figure it out?''

"I think she came to see that she could do more for the animals with ordinary philanthropy. After my husband died, for instance, Ophelia donated a new wing to the city pound in his name.''

"And she quit the group?''

"I'm not sure, Nick. Certainly she became less visibly active.''

"Is she still interested in animal rights?" he asked.

"She still won't eat meat or wear leather or furs, whether or not she goes to COGPAR meetings. I think these days she spends most of her time on the children. And art and music.''

"Art and music. Right."

He closed his eyes for a moment and rested, and experienced the flowers, which smelled. When he opened his eyes again the old lady was bending over him, frowning, with a very serious and earnest face.

"Nick, I want you to tell me something," she said. "Be honest. Do you really think that one of my family could be responsible for these poisonings?"

It was Nick's turn to decide whether to ladle out the old hoo-ha or to trust his friend enough to tell her the bald truth. He decided to trust her.

"Hettie," he confessed, "I haven't a clue."

Buddy Pollert may have appeared to be a mere lab assistant, but he considered himself to be a young man on the make. And actually he was, sort of.

He was consumed by ambitions. He wanted to be a veterinarian. He went to night school, but sometimes he couldn't seem to get to class, what with one thing and another, and at other times the teachers didn't grade his work as high as he deserved and he never could bring his average above a C.

He wanted to be president of the company. But all the daughters were taken. And twenty years his senior in any case. Not that he didn't like older women; for some reason they didn't like him.

He wanted to be admired and respected. So he took drugs.

It worked fine for about half an hour. He was king of the heap. But after the effect wore off his self-esteem went too, and he started making mental lists of ways to save himself, ways to assume his rightful place in the world. In this world, and sometimes in the next.

After he wrecked his car he had trouble commuting. He began sleeping at Porcpharm now and then. There was a shower there and everything, even a little washer-dryer to do his clothes so he didn't have to smell like a bum. With the lab coats and all, nobody seemed to notice or care that he always wore the same things.

After the poisonings began they started locking up the cafeteria food at night and the employees stopped keeping things to eat in their desks. He lived on fruit and monkey chow. It tasted all right. There wasn't any reason to go back to his apartment.

But if only he could get promoted somehow or transfer full time to the animal labs, then he could get Dr. Gagne off his back and life would be nearly perfect. Here she was, after him again. She was signed on to the computer terminal and apparently she had come across something she didn't like.

"Buddy!" she called. "I thought the teratology studies on hivostatin were carried out months ago."

He came over to her desk, squinted at the terminal display and sweated a little. "Teratology studies?" he said.

"You and Dr. Gables took care of that, right? Or I thought you did. Certainly I told you to. And yet I find no record of it here."

Luckily he had a message for her on an entirely different subject. "There's a guy outside waiting to see you," he said.

"If it's that man from the new owners, he can't come in here without an authorization from Howard. I told him that already. Supra Labs doesn't legally own this place until the government approves the merger."

"No, it's some lawyer," he said. "Here's his card." It

was a business card bearing the name of Howells Gould, attorney-at-law.

She looked at the card, frowning. "We'll soon see about *this,*" she muttered. Buddy felt sort of sorry for Howells Gould.

She went out into the vestibule, where the lawyer waited, oily and slightly overfed in a gray pin-striped suit. In his right hand, glittering with gold and diamond rings, he held an envelope. Buddy watched their conversation, although he couldn't hear it through the thick glass. She greeted him, without offering her hand or smiling. He spoke to her, a long speech, his eyes cast down like an undertaker's. Without removing its contents, he flourished the envelope at her.

The back of her neck turned very red. She pointed at the door. He left.

She came back in the lab. For a long time she seemed very preoccupied and forgot about the teratology studies. At least for now.

After Jonathan Fine had solved all Magaracz's problems for nothing, taught him a few t'ai chi moves, and loaded him up with business cards, Concetta came in and took the IV out of his arm.

Time to get out of this bed. Past time. Somebody had hung his second-best suit in the closet. There was a clean shirt, socks, and underwear in the drawer by the bed. He got dressed and then called his wife.

"Ethel, I'm getting out of here. Is my car still at Porcpharm?"

"Sure. Are you okay, Nick?"

"Never felt better."

"Don't do anything stupid, Nick."

"I'm fine. Thanks for the clean clothes, by the way."

"The ones you had on were all messed up. I took the suit to the cleaner's."

"Thanks. I'll see you tonight. I'll take a cab from here to the office."

"Do you think you could eat some lasagna?"

"You bet."

"Call me from work if you're going to be late."

"Right. See you, sweetheart."

"Bye, Nick. Take care."

He fought off their attempts to drive him to the door in a wheelchair, although the chair would have been helpful in trucking out the floral tributes, and settled his affairs with the business office. Somehow he managed to compress the flowers into the back seat of a taxicab, which bore him to his car in the lot at Porcpharm. Nicholas Magaracz, Agent of Industrial Espionage, was back in business.

Twelve

J ared Baines came into Howard's office at nine-thirty. "I've left you till last," he said to Howard. "But what I need from you is a list of the people who report to you, ranked in order of effectiveness."

"I see," Howard said.

"You can't make an omelet without breaking eggs, Howard."

"Of course not."

"It shouldn't take long. I'll be back in ten minutes."

"Okay."

"Monday is the day, you know."

"Yes."

"The takeover becomes final."

"Right."

"I'll see you later." He went out of the office, and Howard focused his mind on that which would make it all worthwhile. Freedom from the cares of Porepharm. Money to do what he wanted. Time to spend with Ophelia, perhaps a month at their place in the islands to start with, away from her clubs and her family, away from everything. The sun, the clear air, the soft sound of azure water lapping against white sand. Blue lizards in the bougainvillea.

Mary broke into his dream to announce Nick Magaracz, freshly arrived from the hospital.

The detective brushed aside Howard's offers of sympathy for the poisoning attempt and immediately began complaining about the maggoty sand pit in the golf course.

"Yes, I know all about that. The health inspector was here and told me someone had called in a complaint. It's been taken care of," Howard said.

"Taken care of?" Magaracz stared at him stupidly, and put a hand on the door frame as if to steady himself. Howard wondered whether he had completely recovered from his attack.

"Yes, yes, taken care of," Howard said. "The grounds crew cleared it away. It was somebody's garbage, somebody who had been picnicking on the grounds."

"You say they cleared it away."

"Why are you harping on this? Nick, it has nothing to do with the poisonings. Nothing. It's just somebody's random garbage. It was unfortunate that the health department became involved. Forget it. It has nothing to do with your job."

The detective drew himself up and began to behave with great pomp. "As an industrial investigator, Howard," he said, "I've found that nothing should be over-looked. Until I put together the big picture, I can't tell what's important." How tiresome the man could be.

"Nick, this is not important. Some of the employees buried the remains of their lunches out there. Fried chicken. I have their names. Letters of reprimand will be placed in their personnel files. Forget it. What you need to do right now is to find out how Arthur Munsen was poisoned."

"Arthur Munsen?" Magaracz looked completely blank.

Howard Strass explained carefully to the detective who Munsen had been, how he was killed in a fall from the atrium balcony, how the coroner had found him to have been drugged. "He was a new employee," Howard said. "He worked in the public relations department. Please get on it."

"Right," said Magaracz. "I'll get right on it." He went away and Howard Strass breathed a long sigh.

But when he left big Howie's office, Nick Magaracz went straight out to the golf course.

The sandbank was neatly squared off. A fair-haired young fellow was standing by his front-end loader, mopping his brow.

"Man," he said. "That ain't a sight I'd want to see every day before lunch."

"What was it?"

"Maggots. Three shovel loads of maggots."

"Well, but what was it? Garbage? Bodies? What?"

"I dunno. Some bones and stuff. Looked almost like babies. I didn't want to look real close."

"Babies!" said Magaracz.

"No, of course it wasn't babies. Big Howie wouldn't have got us to take dead babies to the dump. Get real."

"What dump?" Magaracz said. He was very interested in getting a look at the so-called garbage.

"I dunno. The dump. How many dumps are there?"

"You got me, buddy. What did you say your friend's name was? The one with the truck?"

"Jose."

"He'll know where he took the maggots, right? I'll ask him. Thanks anyhow." Magaracz noticed then that there seemed to be paths through the long grass of the golf course, one of them leading up the hill behind Porcpharm. Arthur Munsen could wait a little longer. He decided to go for a walk in the woods.

The path was narrow, little more than a disturbance of the underbrush, and Magaracz realized that it must have been a deer track. Here and there a muddy place revealed the print of a split hoof. He stopped and looked back. Porcpharm and its surrounding grounds looked like an architect's drawing, a gray building whose wings jutted at crazy angles, set among gray parking lots in a big golden field. The maintenance worker was sitting on the tread of his front-end loader, tiny and far away, drinking from a thermos.

Magaracz thought, *If I sit up here long enough, say with a pair of binoculars, I can see everything that happens.* But that wasn't really true. What he could do from up there was keep himself from getting poisoned again. He really didn't like getting poisoned. He turned back toward the hill and struggled upwards a few more yards, when there on the trail he saw a big bloodstain.

Yes, that's what it was, a bloodstain. Here was a scene of violent death: Dried blood and broken branches, and the track of a large body seemingly dragged away. *You wouldn't think,* Magaracz reflected, *that so much violence could happen right here on the outskirts of Princeton.*

But of course this wasn't your regular violence. This was hunting. Even one with as little woodcraft as Nick could see the deer hair caught on the twigs.

A ring of empty pint whiskey bottles encircled a large tree. Ten feet up in a tree was a platform the size of a small tabletop, overlooking the deer trail. How far could you see from up there? Magaracz decided to climb on up and have a look. Sticks had been nailed to the tree as footholds. The platform seemed good and solid. The view of old Porcineau's golf course would be nearly unobstructed. Putting his head up over the edge, Magaracz found himself looking down the twin barrels of a shotgun that rested on the knees of a hunter sitting with his back against the tree trunk.

The man's eyes bored into his. "Whaddeya want?" he said.

Magaracz backed down hastily. "Some information," he called. "I'm looking for somebody saw something here last week, maybe the week before. You been here long?"

"I ain't been here no two weeks," the man said.

"Did you kill a deer here last week?" said Magaracz.

"What's it to you, buddy? You a game warden?"

"Do I look like a game warden?" said Magaracz. The guy hung his head over the side of the platform and checked him out.

No person who could see clearly had ever accused Magaracz of looking like a game warden in his second-best suit. Of course, he didn't usually go out in the woods wearing it. Maybe this guy wasn't seeing well.

Maybe that had something to do with the empty pint bottle of Old Forester he was throwing out of the tree.

Magaracz said, "I'm trying to find somebody who might have been here when something happened, somebody who might have seen something. Did you notice anything unusual on the Porcpharm grounds, down in the valley? Somebody burying stuff?"

"So you're not a game warden, you're a cop."

"Were you up there last week? I'm not a cop. Listen, I'll buy you another bottle of Old Forester."

The sound of a deep sigh issued from the platform. "I hunt with a gun," said the man. "I don't hunt with no bow and arrow. Last week was bow season. This week is regular season. Okay?"

"So you're telling me that last week somebody up here shot a deer using a bow and arrow."

"He would have to, wouldn't he?" said the man. "Last week it wasn't gun season. Now get lost, Jack. And don't touch nothing. Your scent is gonna scare the deer."

Magaracz hiked back down the hill again, and took another look at the gaping hole in old Porcineau's sand trap. It told him nothing. He checked in with the maintenance department on his way back to his office, but they told him that Jose had not come back from the dump.

"What dump was it?" he asked.

"I dunno," said the girl. "The dump. Whatever dump would let him in."

That could be a number of places, or no place, the state of trash disposal in New Jersey being what it was. Another thing to track down. Legwork. How he hated it. He went back to his office, where he found that the phone was ringing.

It was Big Howie.

"Before I let the maintenance staff clean out Arthur Munsen's office," said Howie, "I thought you should get a look at his things."

"Right," said Magaracz. "Yes. Certainly." Munsen. Right.

Munsen's office was two corridors away from Magaracz's own, with the other offices of the public relations department. Unlike Magaracz, Munsen had no window; probably this fact had some political significance.

Munsen hadn't occupied the office very long. It had few of the encrustations of personal memorabilia that tend to collect in a guy's office as the years roll by. In the desk drawer, Magaracz turned up some raffle tickets—Munsen had been a soft touch, evidently—a sparkling clean ashtray and some business correspondence. On the wall, a calendar with two dentist appointments and the birthday of someone named Shirley marked on it. On the desk, more papers, a dictionary, and a copy of *The Chicago Manual of Style,* all piled on top of a large desk blotter.

But under this, tucked into the corner of the blotter, was a five-by-seven glossy print of Dr. Margaret Gagne, sitting under a tree in the atrium. What was it that this woman had for all these men? Magaracz himself couldn't see it, and it wasn't only because she wasn't his type. There was something repellent about her, something in her eyes.

This particular picture had been doodled on with a blue ballpoint pen, the way you might draw a moustache on a picture in the newspaper. What had been done to it was this:

Cascading curly hair had been squiggled all over the

head and down the shoulders. Luxuriant eyelashes had been drawn on the eyes. A Cupid's bow had been added to the thin lips. Bulbous breasts with nipples had been superimposed on the austere lab coat. A crotch and pubic hair had been sketched in the appropriate area. And underneath, a caption had been added:

FLEUR DU MAL

By God, this was a clue if ever Magaracz had seen one.

Of course, it could have been planted.

What did it mean?

Thirteen

Dr. Margaret Gagne marched unannounced into the office of Howard Strass. This she had not done in more than a year, and he looked up in surprise and pleasure. But the look on her face was all business.

"Your brother-in-law is at it again," she said without preamble.

"Oh—what—" With both hands he rubbed his head. Carl was certainly a difficult person.

"A whole battery of studies on hivostatin has been completely bypassed. Either bypassed or erased from the computer files."

"What makes you think that Carl—?"

"Just because you two have fixed it up between you so that I never go into the animal labs, you seem to think that I won't keep track of the tests on my own drugs. I'm telling you, Howard, Carl Gables is either malfeasant or criminally negligent on this one and I'm going to nail his ass to the wall, relative or no relative. Are you with me or against me?"

He gazed out the window at the parking lot. A maintenance man was gripping the sign that marked his personal spot, HOWARD STRASS, PRESIDENT, and wrenching it from side to side, working it out of the frozen ground. Three more days here. "I'm against you, Margaret. I have to be. I mean, can't you let this go, please, for another three days? Just three days. It isn't very long."

She looked surprised and offended. She said, "I see that you know already what I'm talking about." She never wore perfume anymore. She used to smell of patchouli, a strange erotic fragrance that could capture his attention from the other side of a room. Now she smelled only of chemicals and a little whiff of body odor.

"Let it go, Margaret. No harm will be done."

"No harm! God *damn* you." She went out. *Wham!* went his office door. His umbrella stand fell over. What she would do next he could scarcely imagine.

Magaracz pursued the case of the murdered deer. He called Jonathan Fine, still in his hospital bed at Princeton Medical Center, and although Fine had no idea who might have killed the deer, he was able to direct Nick Magaracz to the local bow and gun shop, where hunting licenses were sold and dead deer were weighed.

The shop was on the main street of Hopewell. There

was a crowd of women outside carrying signs and
wearing plaid skirts, boiled wool jackets, and sneakers.
Magaracz realized they were picketing the place. The
protesting group was none other than COGPAR, itself,
Citizens of Greater Princeton for Animal Rights, the
group that had gotten Ophelia Porcineau Strass to embarrass her family. As he made his way inside, some of
the women in the group called him a murderer in low
well-bred voices.

Magaracz himself did not like guns, but if he had
been inclined that way, there were some nice ones
behind the glass counter, and some powerful-looking
compound bows as well. The arrowheads they used on
the deer looked almost like ninja weapons. Bunches of
razor blades. The guy sold a thing called an arrowhead
wrench whose sole purpose was to enable you to screw
the killer arrowheads onto their shafts without slicing
all your fingers off. No wonder Fine had to be hospital-
ized, if he shot himself with one of those things.

The women were beginning to chant. Magaracz
could hear their voices through the door, but not what
they were saying. "How long has that gang been out
there?" he asked the proprietor, by way of starting a
conversation.

"Too long," the man replied lugubriously. "Weeks."

"I guess they can make it tough on anybody who
brings a dead deer in."

The proprietor smiled. "Well, now, there we've been
lucky. That crowd usually turns up for a couple of
hours in the afternoon, and all the deer I've had to
weigh have been shot at sundown or in the early morning."

"There was one killed a week or two ago," said

Magaracz. "I need to find the guy who shot him. Bow hunter. I wonder if you could help me out."

"What do you want him for?" the proprietor said.

"Nothing bad," said Magaracz. "I think he might have seen something, and I need to know what, is all."

"You a cop?"

"Private investigator."

"Oh, hanky-panky in the woods, eh? Kind of cold for that." The man gave him a broad wink.

"Never too cold," said Magaracz, winking back. "What do you say? Can you help me find this guy?"

The proprietor was extremely cooperative, and after quizzing Magaracz about the nature and location of the kill gave him the name and address of Oscar Willingham, a customer of his who had come in the week before last with a large buck he had bagged with bow and arrow. He even offered Magaracz a cup of coffee. Magaracz declined with thanks and went out the door, only to be surrounded by the animal rights activists again.

"I'm shocked," he said to them. "That man has guns in there."

The women exchanged suspicious glances. Was he putting them on?

"No, really," said Nick. "I'm interested in your work. I'm a friend of Ophelia Strass."

While some fumbled in their canvas tote bags for leaflets another simply muttered, "How sympathetic could he be? He's wearing leather shoes."

At the mention of Ophelia's name, the tall one with iron-gray hair drew herself up a little taller. "Mrs. Strass is no longer with COGPAR," she said. "Family loyalty was more important to her, evidently, than the lives and welfare of the animals in her family's care. I can understand what happened. The Porcineaus are very close."

"No guts," said the little malcontent.

"You might remind her when you see her," said the one with the gold-rimmed glasses, "to give us back our Polaroid camera."

"She has your camera?" said Magaracz.

"She went out after last month's meeting with COG-PAR's Polaroid to get photographic evidence of conditions at Porcineau Pharmaceuticals," the gray-haired woman said. "But she never came back. In fact, we haven't heard a word from her since that night."

"I was disappointed in her, myself," said gold-rim. "I thought she was ready. Remember how resolute she seemed, dressed all in black with that cute beret?"

"Ophelia is nothing if not a stylist," the little one said.

"She did keep the camera," said the gray-haired woman to Magaracz. "I'm sure it was an oversight; I'd be grateful if you would mention it to her when you see her. It might be that she doesn't realize its value to us."

"Okay," said Magaracz. "I'll be sure and tell her."

"I must admit that the whole episode was a mistake in judgment on my part," the gray-haired woman said. "I never should have sent her to photograph her own family's animal laboratories. Tell her hello for us when you see her. Tell her I'm sorry and I don't blame her. Any time she wants to rejoin a group that makes a true statement of her real ideals and feelings, there's still a place for her at COGPAR. Tell her that."

He promised, and then he accepted a handful of brochures and returned to his office.

*   *   *

Willingham was in the telephone book and by chance was at home when Nick called. He was happy to tell his story. He laid it on thick, the break of dawn, his frozen limbs, the bobbing light suddenly appearing on the Porcpharm grounds. When he got to the part where a mysterious figure was struggling with a box, Magaracz asked him, "Could there have been a body in it?"

"No way," said the hunter. "This is a wimpy little guy, he couldn't have carried a shovel and a body both in the same trip. It was a small box, anyhow."

"The size of a breadbox."

"A breadbox. Yeah. Don't you think I would have called the cops if I thought it was a body?"

"Sure. No offense. You get a good look at him?"

"Yeah. The sky was starting to get light. He was wearing a white coat. It made him easier to see. Like I said, he was this little guy, stooped over, chicken chest, stringy hair, bad acne—you know him?"

"I think so."

"So what was in the box?"

"We're not sure."

"Drugs?"

Magaracz hadn't thought of drugs. But, no, not with the flies. "No way of knowing," he said. "So you saw this guy pushing a box across the golf course."

"Yeah, he pushes it, then he picks it up and carries it a little way, then he drags it, and so on. It didn't look very heavy, just awkward to carry."

"Then what happened?"

"Then I heard leaves rustling, and I looked down, and here came this eight-point buck. I want to tell you, that baby was in deep, dark trouble." He went on to describe in great detail the dispatching of the buck, its death throes, the difficulty he had getting it out of the woods, how much meat it yielded, and all the other things that made the incident interesting to him, if not to Nick Magaracz. The detective thanked him for his time.

Outside the office window, the wind had picked up, and a nasty little freezing rain was falling. The trees that Porepharm's gardeners had planted in the parking lot were lashing to and fro like shaken mops. Glare ice was visible in patches on the roadway. Driving home was going to be tough. Maybe it would warm up before he had to scrape the Thunderbird's windshield.

The hunter's little wimp was surely none other than Buddy Pollert. Interesting. Wasn't it Pollert who claimed to have tested Howard's poison samples? How easily he could have faked the outcome of those tests. It was mid-morning; that would put him in the chem labs about now. Magaracz left his office and headed for the back stairs that led to the chemistry lab.

Then suddenly the building's lights went out. Someone had skidded into a light pole.

A shocked silence, and then an outcry, heard all up and down the halls. Some grunted, some cursed, some said, "Oh." There were a few cheers. Workers whose offices had no windows came out into the halls, groping like dungeon inmates.

Magaracz headed across the building to the atrium, where there was natural light to climb the stairs by. Others were gathering there, some talking together, some smoking, waiting for the lights to come on.

Gazing out over the balcony Magaracz saw a familiar face, the face of Kevin Mandelbaum, the social worker.

"Kevin," he said to the guy. "How's it going?"

"Pretty good. Nick Magaracz, isn't it? Wow, it's been a long time," he said. He looked a bit more kempt than he had when Magaracz saw him last. The beard was neatly trimmed. The shoes were shined. "What brings you here? Porcpharm forget to pay their sales tax?"

"I don't work for the state anymore," said Nick. "I'm in industrial investigations. How about you? I saw your leaflet on the bulletin board. You working for Porcpharm?"

"Sure," he grinned. "That is, I work for New Life Systems. They contract my services to Porcineau Pharmaceuticals as an employee benefit."

"Solving the problems of the yuppies," Magaracz said.

"Beats trying to help the poor, Nick. I want to tell you, it's a whole other ball game working with middle-class people."

"Oh," said Magaracz, in as neutral a voice as he could manage. Still Mandelbaum bristled with defensiveness. Apparently it was an issue he had not resolved in his own soul.

He said, "I've paid my dues. Yuppies need help like anybody else. Debt counseling, drug and alcohol counseling, grief therapy, marriage counseling, all kinds of things."

"You bet," said Magaracz.

The social worker pulled back a lock of hair to reveal a white scar on his forehead about an inch long. "See that? That was my last case working for the county. I had to take a child out of an abusive home situation. The father did that with a brick. Five stitches. I don't owe the poor a damned thing."

People were always showing him their scars, with virtually no provocation. It was strange. "You're looking good, Kevin. How's Monica? I think of her sometimes."

"We're not together any more, Nick. She dumped me. For a fifty-year-old chief of police, would you believe."

"Go figure women," said Magaracz, although he wasn't really surprised. Monica always struck him as one of these dames that would go for the Rambo type sooner than a sensitive guy like Kevin. He was better off. "You want to have lunch? We can meet in the cafeteria."

"Thanks, Nick, but I brought my lunch."

"Right. So did I. It's okay to eat there if you bring your own lunch. I'll see you at noon."

"Okay, then, noon it is," said Mandelbaum.

That would just give Magaracz time to confront Buddy Pollert, make him confess to burying the babies, force him to reveal where they came from, turn the case over to the police, and call Ethel, with ten minutes to spare for running to the convenience store for a cup of coffee. Better get on it. He headed up the stairs and out into the dark hallway.

At the end of the hall he could see the red glow of the light on the chemistry lab's lock. Daylight showed under the door. Probably they were still working away in there. The guard lurking in the dark buzzed the intercom—battery-operated, evidently—and asked for Buddy Pollert.

"He's down in the animal labs," a man's voice said.

There wouldn't be any light there. An image formed in Magaracz's mind of cage doors opening, dark shapes creeping out. Wracked with premonitions, Magaracz nearly had another drug flashback before he finished groping his way to the bottom of the subbasement stairs.

The guard had a flashlight turned on at his desk. He shined it on Nick's face. "Pollert in there?" Nick asked.

"Must be," said the guard. "He hasn't come out. I don't know what he's doing, all alone in the dark."

"Where's Dr. Gables?" said Magaracz. "Where are the other lab assistants?"

"The women all went to lunch early," said the guard. "A baby shower or something. Dr. Gables didn't come in today." He punched the combination on the lock. It too must have run on batteries; the door swung open. "Hey!" called the guard. "Buddy Pollert?"

Only the grunts and squeals of the animals answered him from the darkness.

"Let me see that flashlight," Magaracz said. The hair on the back of his neck was rising up. He shined the light around, on the rat cages, on the rabbits. They ran around restlessly, making scuttling noises.

Then as suddenly as they had gone off the lights came on again, blinding them both for a moment. When the blindness passed Pollert was revealed stretched out stone dead on a stainless-steel table.

This was getting depressing.

How did he die? The coffee again? Or did one of the apes hit him a whack as he passed the cages? And how did he get on the table?

Only the monkeys knew for sure.

Fourteen

The investigating officers seemed skeptical when Magaracz told them the remains that Jose had taken to the dump had a very important bearing on this case. He told them the whole story three times, and they just stared at him as if to say "Who the hell are you?" It's tough to work away from your own turf. Nobody respects you.

But he persisted. They promised to check it out. If Burton Pollert had buried dead babies on old Porcineau's golf course it could help to explain why he was killed.

Finally they thanked him for his statement and sent him away. He went to meet Kevin Mandelbaum in the company cafeteria.

Operations in the cafeteria had been suspended for an indefinite period. What with one thing and another, hardly anybody would eat there anymore. It didn't pay to keep it open. Employees of Porcineau Pharmaceuticals were allowed to use the tables and napkins for their own bag lunches.

Men and women were hunched singly or in groups of two or three, eating furtively, sitting as far as possible from one another. Nobody laughed or talked very loud. Magaracz found Kevin Mandelbaum eating a big piece of pita bread with sprouts or something dribbling out of it.

"This place is weird," remarked Magaracz.

"Too true," said Mandelbaum. "You should see my caseload."

"I bet you know everything that goes on around here," said Magaracz.

"If it goes wrong, and people are suffering over it, I usually hear about it," he said. "For instance, three of the women in production and manufacturing had miscarriages last month. First of all they needed counseling to help them cope, but secondly they all plan to sue. They think it's one of the drugs they're working on."

"Can't the union do anything?" said Magaracz.

"Union!" he laughed. "What union? You are living in the past, Nick. Yuppies don't do union."

"Listen," said Magaracz. "Do the words 'Fleur du Mal' mean anything to you?"

"Sure," said Mandelbaum. He swallowed a bite of health sandwich. "Flowers of evil. It's the title of a poem by Baudelaire."

"Hm," said Magaracz. "No, that can't be it. What does the poem say?"

"Nothing much," said Mandelbaum. "Just how rotten everything is and how we're all to blame or something. Why do you ask?"

"No reason. I heard it somewhere. So what else is up with the troops at Porcpharm?"

"They're afraid of getting poisoned," said Mandelbaum "or they're afraid of getting fired, or they're suffering stress generally. I get the feeling talking to them that Porcpharm isn't the best place in the world to be working these days. How about you, Nick? Aren't you afraid of getting fired?"

"Nah. I wouldn't mind it. And I got poisoned already."

"You're the guy!" said Mandelbaum. "I heard something about that. What happened, anyway? You wouldn't believe some of the stories going around. You were actually poisoned? Did you recover okay?"

"Sort of," said Magaracz. "Sometimes I feel more recovered than other times. I drank some bad coffee; I passed out; they stuck me in the hospital for a couple days. I still see things."

"Things?"

"Things that ain't there," Magaracz said darkly. "I been on the plane of existence."

"Oh. Well, people were saying you died, or you went crazy. . . . Who gave you the poison?"

"Big Howie," said Magaracz. "If there was a union here we'd really have a case, huh?"

"Big Howie? No shit," said Mandelbaum. "This is worse than I thought. So that's how he's cutting the work force."

"I don't think he did it on purpose," said Magaracz. "Is he cutting the work force?"

"They announced a twenty percent cut. That's

about three hundred people. Nobody has been tapped
yet."

"What do you tell people when they come to you for
help?"

"I refer them to an employment counselor in our
group. She helps them write résumés. Did you notice
that all the coffee machines have been removed?"

"It came to my attention," he said.

"Everybody brings a thermos now and locks it in the
desk. And yet they're having an awards dinner here
tonight."

"In the cafeteria?"

"In the atrium," he said. "Didn't you hear about it?"

"No, I've been away on my plane trip," said Magaracz. "Do you know this guy, by any chance?" He
pushed Jonathan Fine's card across the table.

Mandelbaum smiled. "Yeah, Jonathan," he said.
"Where did you run into him?"

"He was in the bed next to me at Princeton Medical
Center."

"What was he in for?"

"Shot himself in the foot."

"No kidding. He used to be so nonviolent."

"He gave me his card because he thinks I need treat-
ment for posttraumatic stress syndrome."

"That's not his specialty. He does mad housewives
and disturbed adolescents."

"Do you think I have posttraumatic stress syndrome?"

"How do you feel about it yourself?" he said.

"I dunno. I feel pretty good. Usually I manage to
suffer as little stress as possible."

"Well, if you find yourself having trouble sleeping,

or crying a lot, or anything like that—maybe having trouble with your relationships—"

But Nick wasn't listening to Mandelbaum at all. He was having an idea. "Do you ever work with deaf people?" he said.

"Sure," said Mandelbaum. "Why?"

"Do you speak—or whatever—sign language?"

"American sign language, sure. It's been almost as useful in my line of work as Spanish."

"I think—Here's the thing." He bent closer and spoke in a low voice. "I think Carl Gables might be teaching sign language to some of those apes down there. If they're witnesses to Buddy Pollert's murder, then maybe . . ."

"Maybe they can tell you something. Sounds like a long shot, Nick. Why don't you get Gables to help you?"

Magaracz gave him a meaningful look. "I get it," said Mandelbaum. "Gables is a suspect. Well then, why trust me?"

"You're not from around here," Magaracz said, grinning. "How about it? You want to help me interrogate the monkeys?"

Fifteen

Magaracz and Mandelbaum crept down the back stairs to the subbasement and found by a stroke of luck that the Haitian guard had stepped away from his post, the cops were gone, and the workers who had left early to attend the shower were still out. Nobody was around at all.

Magaracz's ever-useful pocket notebook yielded the combination to the door that led to the animal lab's outer vestibule. It was necessary to pick the lock on a second door to reach the animals. Carl Gables's office door was the easiest. Kevin Mandelbaum seemed either horrified or impressed, it was hard to tell. "You do a lot of this?" he said.

"Only when all else fails," said Magaracz. "There." The lock came open. They went into the tidy office.

"Obsessive-compulsive," said Mandelbaum, with a glance at the empty surfaces. "A clean desk is the sign of a sick mind. It's true." The door to the laboratory was not locked from the office side.

"Let's prop it open," said Magaracz. The door seemed to have been installed to open from one side only, as a precaution against escape attempts by clever ape hands; only a key could work the laboratory side. Mandelbaum put a chair against it and they stepped into the lab.

The lights in the animal laboratory were so bright that the effect was almost the same as that of darkness; the eye was confused, objects obscured, no clue given as to whether it was day or night outside in the world. In a word, it was creepy. Magaracz hoped to get them in and out fast, before . . .

"Oh, wow," said Kevin Mandelbaum. "Wow."

"What?" said Magaracz, jumping nervously, looking over his shoulder and all around.

"I never realized," said Mandelbaum. "All these animals in cages."

"What did you think it was like? Don't any of your clients work down here?"

"Not that I know of," the social worker said.

"Figures," said Magaracz. "Probably anyone who could work down here is so far gone in weirdness that he's past help."

"It just . . . it blows my mind, man. How can they do this? And they infect them with germs and give them drugs and everything. And afterwards . . ."

"I know five ladies in Princeton who would like to have you in their club," said Magaracz. "It's called COGPAR."

Mandelbaum knelt down by the cages and offered his finger to a bunny to sniff and nibble.

"Better not," said Magaracz. "No telling what that little guy might give you."

Mandelbaum recoiled. "It's criminal," he said. "Poor things. I mean, think of it. People peddle these bits of life the way you'd sell any commodity." Magaracz felt sorry for him. Bleeding heart. He was suffering on behalf of every white mouse and fruit fly in the room.

"But farmers have done that for thousands of years," said Magaracz. "Raising animals for commercial purposes. Nobody says, 'How terrible.' "

"I do," said Mandelbaum. "Or did you think I ate meat?"

Magaracz sighed. What he wanted right now was a good big feed of Hungarian stuffed cabbage. With meat. Rich meaty juices. "Let's see if we can talk to these monkeys," he said.

They went straight to the ape cages, stepping around the steel table with its body-shaped chalk mark where Magaracz had found Buddy Pollert. Magaracz figured that, first of all, you had to have hands to do sign language, and secondly you had to have something like human intelligence, so the great apes were their best bet.

Treasure, the first she-ape they came to, was unresponsive to Kevin Mandelbaum's waggling and gesturing. So were the others they tried. But in the last cage they found Jewel. When they approached her she seemed to perk up considerably, left off chewing the bark of a big stick in her cage and came to the bars with something that might have passed for a congenial smile.

The transcription that they made of the ensuing exchange reads like this:

Mandelbaum:	Hello.
Jewel:	Hello.
Mandelbaum:	Man fall here today.
Jewel:	Candy. Give.
Mandelbaum:	See man fall?
Jewel:	Give candy.
Mandelbaum:	Someone hit man?
Jewel:	Give candy now.
Mandelbaum:	Jewel see man get hit?
Jewel:	Now give Jewel candy.
Mandelbaum:	Who hit man?
Jewel:	Give much candy.
Mandelbaum:	Man fall. Jewel hit man? Ape hit man?
Jewel:	Jewel want much candy.
Mandelbaum:	Somebody hit man. Man fall on table. Jewel see?
Jewel:	Give.

Finally Nick got a Snickers bar from the vending machine in the vestibule and gave it to Jewel. She accepted the gift and retired with it to a far corner of her cage, where she grasped it in her right foot, peeling the wrapping off and picking out the peanuts with the fingers of her hands. Consuming the Snickers bar absorbed the ape's entire attention after that and she refused to engage in further communication with the humans.

"Well, I wrote it all down," said Mandelbaum, "And now I'm signing and dating it. Do you think it's any use?"

"None whatever," said the detective. Of course, he now knew which monkey could communicate in sign language. But he couldn't see where the information might be useful. "But save it anyway," he said. "Maybe it'll come in handy."

On his desk was yet another message to call Howie Strass.

Howie said, "I forgot to tell you this morning, but we're having an awards dinner tonight and I need you to be there to make sure nobody gets poisoned."

"How? You want me to try all the food, or what?"

"Nick, I really need you to do this for me. There won't be any danger. You don't have to eat or drink anything suspicious, just watch to be sure that nobody from Porcpharm slips anything into the stuff the caterer is bringing."

"I'm supposed to do this by myself? What about the regular security staff?"

"Two men from security will be there. But I particularly want you, Nick. As an outsider." *Right*, thought Nick. *I'm not from around here.*

"Okay," he said. "And that reminds me. Do the words 'Fleur du mal' mean anything to you?"

"French, isn't it?" said Howard.

"I guess so."

"No, it doesn't mean a thing to me. I studied German, myself. Why do you ask?"

"No reason," said Magaracz.

"How did you make out with Arthur Munsen's office?" said Howard. "Find anything useful?"

"Not to speak of," said Magaracz.

Howard Strass said, "See you tonight then. Six-thirty in the atrium."

Magaracz said, "Right, six-thirty," and hung up, and then he put in a call to the local police, asking to speak to the officer who was handling the case of Burton Pollert's death.

The officer told him that they had been unable to locate Jose the maintenance man. In spite of that, they were pursuing the search for whatever it was that Burton Pollert had buried. Jose's relatives reported that he had come into some money and had suddenly gone to rejoin an old girlfriend in Puerto Rico.

"Sounds almost like hush money, doesn't it?" said Magaracz.

"Mr. Magaracz, I have to agree that it seems suspicious," the lieutenant said. "I have a man searching a couple of the dumps right now. Give me a call again later and I'll let you know if we turn anything up."

Magaracz hung up, and suddenly he thought, *babies*. Illegitimate issue of local love affairs, involving people in the company. What nubile females were working at Porcpharm? According to the personnel files, there could be several hundred of them.

Why would Strass want to cover it up? Which is what he was clearly doing.

Horrific images assailed his mind of someone, Margaret Gagne maybe, secretly giving birth to twins unattended in the dark of night on the premises of Porcineau Pharmaceuticals, strangling them, getting Buddy Pollert to bury them, killing everybody to hush the whole thing up. For a moment he thought the drug flashbacks were going to get him again. To clear his head he turned his thoughts to Arthur Munsen, whose personnel file was on the desk in front of him.

The file contained Munsen's picture. Magaracz recognized him as the wretch who had got the last cup of
unpoisoned coffee in the company kitchen. Or was it
unpoisoned? Maybe even that cup was doctored, waiting for Magaracz himself to drink it and die. Munsen's
bad luck. His résumé revealed that he had worked for
the commissioner of higher education before Porcpharm, and before that ten years as a reporter for the
Trentonian.

There was a bar in Trenton where the local newsmen
liked to gather. Magaracz had heard you could get a
good home-cooked feed there, Hungarian food and
everything. Maybe somebody there would want to talk
about Arthur Munsen. Meanwhile Magaracz could get
something to eat before this so-called dinner of
Howie's, in a place where with any luck nobody would
try to poison him.

Heading out to his car, Magaracz saw the raven
again by the side of the drive and this time he was able
to get a good look at what the bird had been pecking
and worrying for the past week.

It was a dead squirrel, run over so many times that
it looked like a furry gray pancake with a tail. No meat
on it or anything. The raven must have eaten all the
good parts. Everywhere you went, dead animals.

Sixteen

Magaracz parked the Thunderbird in the city lot on Front Street. Maybe he would get lucky and somebody would steal Ophelia's flowers. The saloon was nearby, next to a state office building and down the street from a Catholic church. If you weren't looking for it, you would hardly know it was there; only the funny-shaped window and a small neon sign identified it as a bar. Magaracz went in and ordered a draft beer.

The proprietor asked, smiling, if he were with the media. He had to confess that he wasn't. Like a lot of bars in Trenton, this one was sort of like a private club.

But then Magaracz was in luck. Salvatore del Pietro, a cousin of Ethel's who had been for many years a reporter—alternately for the *Trentonian* and the *Eve-*

ning Times of Trenton—was sitting at the other end
of the bar having a corned beef sandwich.

"Sal," said Magaracz. "How's it going?"

"Good," said the reporter.

Now to pump him for gossip about Art Munsen,
thought Magaracz. On a whim he decided to ask him
the tough question first.

"What do you know about Fleur du Mal?"

"Greatest body I ever saw," said the reporter, not
even pausing to think.

Magaracz was nonplussed. "What?"

"Topless go-go dancer. Used to play the Singing
Sands, years ago. Wonder what ever happened to her.
She's in the men's room. laM ud ruelF."

"Come again?"

"You've never seen the men's room here," said Sal.

"No," Magaracz admitted. "Can't say I have."

"You should." Sal went on to explain how some
years ago the *Trentonian* had changed over from letterpress to offset lithography. A regular item on the
entertainment page in those days used to be a full-
length picture of the featured go-go dancer of the week
at one or another of the local joints, one column wide
by about three inches high, wearing her working
clothes and a big friendly smile.

In the letterpress process, in order to put such a
picture in the paper, a cut had to be made, a stiff metal
casting of the picture with the shading represented by
tiny dots. The picture appeared reversed, and all writing was backwards. The *Trentonian* saved these cuts
in their library to reuse whenever a particular dancer
was featured again.

"When they went to offset, they had no more use for

the cuts they had been saving. They were going to throw them all out. All that pulchritude."

". . . and so?"

"The cuts were all the same size and shape, like tiles. Some of us brought them over here and grouted them to the bathroom wall," said Sal. The proprietor grinned and continued to polish the bar.

"Strippers," Magaracz said.

"Why not? They're very decorative."

"laM ud ruelF."

"And eiduN ycnaN, and ddaB eisteB. I even have rraB ydnaC. She played Trenton one time. But go and see for yourself."

He did. They had pasted the cuts to one wall, the way you would lay ceramic tile, and it made a very nice effect. Nobody had written anything on them. laM ud ruelF was right at eye level, hard to miss, but to Magaracz she looked pretty much like all the others with the smile and the fringed costume. He went back out again.

"Nice," he said. "Tell me something." He withdrew the five-by-seven glossy with the ballpoint-pen marks from his inside breast pocket. "Could this be our girl laM?"

"God," Sal breathed. "It sure could. What is she now, a dental assistant? Where did you get this?"

"Give it back. It's evidence."

"Of what?"

"The ravages of time, my son," said Magaracz, pocketing the picture. "The ravages of time. But what I really need to know about is Arthur Munsen."

"I heard he was dead," said Sal. "He used to go out with Fleur."

"No kidding," said Magaracz.

"His wife never knew about it," Sal said. "Don't mention it to anybody."

"Right," said Magaracz, and ordered a plate of stuffed cabbage.

While his cabbage was heating up Magaracz made a call from the public phone in the bar to the officer in charge of investigating Pollert's death to check on how they were coming with the search for the dead babies.

"We found them," said the officer. "But we aren't talking about human remains here."

"Was it fried chicken?" said Magaracz, his heart sinking.

"No. It was not fried chicken. We took it to a veterinarian this morning and what she said it was was the partial remains of three infant apes, just the heads and torsos. There is definitely a public health problem involved here. It remains to be seen whether or not we can file charges against Porcineau Pharmaceuticals."

Monkey babies.

So what was the story? Why were the bodies in the sand trap?

What was Howard Strass trying to hide?

His cabbage steaming fragrantly on the corner table, Magaracz made one more call, this time to Big Howie. Sometimes when you talked to a guy over the telephone it was easier to tell when he was lying.

But Howie was out. Mary Mavis said he had left early to go to the reception.

"What reception?"

"They're opening a new exhibit at the Trenton Art Museum."

"Where?"

"Ellarslie. You must know where it is, Mr. Magaracz, you were a Trenton boy; it's in Cadwallader Park."

"Oh, right," said Nick. "The monkey house."

"They don't like you to call it that anymore," she said. Mrs. Mavis was evidently one of that crowd that wanted Trenton to go upscale.

"Right," he said. "Sorry." He thanked her and hung up, returning to the cabbage. It was very good. He hadn't had a decent meal, he realized, in almost a week.

There was a newspaper on the chair beside him. He checked the local events page, and sure enough there was a wine and cheese party from four to six at Ellarslie, as they now called the old mansion that had been used as a zoo for the city's monkeys during the years when Nick was growing up. He hadn't been back there since the monkeys left, what with one thing and another.

He called Ethel. "I won't be home for supper," he said. "I have to go over to the monkey house and then there's a dinner at Porcpharm that Howard wants me to cover."

"The monkey house?" she said. "What do you want to go there for? Isn't it some kind of an art gallery these days?"

"Yeah. Hettie Porcineau is giving them a million dollars worth of art and they're having a reception. I'm going to try to talk to Howard before this dinner."

"Don't eat anything at Porcpharm," she said.

"I ate already. If I get hungry again maybe I'll get some wine and cheese at the reception."

"Well, be careful, honey," she said. "And don't get mugged." Ethel had these funny ideas about the city.

Seventeen

In the late afternoon twilight, Cadwallader Park hardly seemed to have changed since the days when Nick and his little friends used to come to tease the bears. Some of the trees were gone, and the rest were bigger. The cannon, the old Swamp Angel that had bombarded Charleston and won the Civil War (or so they said) seemed to have been vandalized, perhaps by vindictive Southerners, but more likely by idle locals. The bears themselves had departed this life some time ago and the bear pit was empty.

He parked the car by the side of the road, under a huge, ancient tree, leafless and creaking. A cold moon struggled out from behind blowing clouds. The old monkey house at the top of the hill looked bright and

116

welcoming. The outdoor cages that once lined its walls were nowhere to be seen. Magaracz went up the walk almost eagerly. Maybe three more questions and he'd have the solution to this whole mess.

At the door, a woman made him pay a couple of dollars to get in. She gave him a big smile and a flyer listing the things that Hester was donating, with pictures of them.

He glanced at the brochure, and stepped inside, and realized that Hester Porcineau was having her little joke.

You had to see the art works in person to get the full effect. They were all apparently by famous artists, museum-quality stuff, and they were all pictures and statues of monkeys.

The first thing he saw was a huge painting, about twice the size of a garage door, of a naked female gorilla. She was lying on her side on a fancy rug, smiling at him with a kind of come-hither look. Nick had seen pictures of women that were sort of like it, only this was a gorilla.

Most of the art lovers were clustered around the wine and cheese, talking about anything except the new art. Ophelia was there and sister Caroline, wining, cheesing, and gassing about some club meeting or other. Nobody wore furs, except for one of the men; probably none of them wanted to offend Ophelia.

Nick found Hester Porcineau standing in front of a display of pencil drawings, a self-satisfied smirk adorning her features. The wig had made a complete recovery from its previous encounter with Trenton culture.

"Very funny, Hetty," said Nick, "but isn't it kind of an expensive joke?"

"I don't know what you mean, Nick," she said

primly. "I hope at my age and station in life I can become a patron of the arts without uncultured louts like you pointing the finger of scorn."

"I wouldn't think of pointing the finger of scorn, Hetty. Where's Howard?"

"He went back to Porcpharm," she said. "There was something he had to take care of before the dinner. You'll be there, won't you?"

"Sure," he said. "Will you?"

"Certainly will," she said. "My last official appearance at Porcpharm. You knew we had sold the company, didn't you?"

"Yeah. I was sort of surprised. Why did you do that? Are you retiring from your business pursuits?"

"No," she said. "Just the drug business."

"I notice that Carl isn't here," Magaracz observed. "Does he ever attend these functions?"

She shrugged. "Not in years," she said. "He's completely wrapped up in his work. He never did go in for culture."

"Something is going on out there," he said. "I came here to find Howard and talk to him about it."

"What is it?" she demanded.

He said, "Hetty, how deeply involved are you in the day-to-day operations of Porcpharm?"

"About as deeply as Carl Gables is involved in my art projects. I haven't touched Porcpharm in ten years, except to attend the board meetings. It was entirely Howard's enterprise. Is something wrong?"

"Somebody buried the heads and torsos of infant monkeys on the Porcpharm grounds." He had spoken louder than he meant to; a lull in conversation among the art lovers caused his words to reverberate.

There was a crash of glassware. Ophelia had

dropped her drink, and was staring at him white-faced from across the room.

For a long minute the gallery seemed to hang in suspended animation. Then the murmur of conversation resumed. Ophelia picked up her coat from a chair by the door and went out. They heard her car starting, scratching off in the gravel.

"Is she all right?" said Magaracz.

"I think so," said Hetty. "She does things like this from time to time."

"Gosh," he said.

"Have some cheese and crackers," the old lady urged. "Take a look at all this art, Nick. Drink some wine. After that you can go chase Howard back to Porcpharm and ask him whatever it is you want to ask him."

Confused and puzzled, he obediently ate some Brie on a thing like a round matzo. "You know, Hetty," he said, "with all the dough you have, I would think you'd get something uplifting for the City of Trenton." It wasn't really the thing that was uppermost in his mind; he was making conversation while his real thoughts percolated.

"Uplifting?" she snorted. "Such as what? These are pretty uplifting. I'll have you know the drawings you're looking at are by Seurat, the great French master of Pointillism."

"I dunno," he said. "The *Venus de Milo* or something."

"Tsk," she said. "At least my monkeys have arms."

Heads and torsos, said a voice in the back of his mind. *No arms or legs.*

And then he realized why the bodies of the infant apes had needed to be hidden.

Eighteen

The full moon shone in the window of Howard's office, so bright as to cast shadows even in the artificial light. Carl Gables stood in the doorway, pleading with Howard. Sweat stood on his upper lip, hair showed above his collar. Howard had a wild thought: *If he steps in here, if he comes into the moonlight, hair will grow even on his face, and his teeth will grow long and pointed, and his nose will become tipped with black leather.*

"Give me the picture," said Carl. "Or burn it here. What use is it to you? If Jared Baines gets hold of it, we'll all be ruined. Or Hester. Can you imagine what she would say? What she would do? Think about it."

He thought about it; it was not pretty. "Oh, all right,

Carl, I can see that you're probably right, I'll give it to you as soon as I get the safe cleaned out. Come back after the awards dinner."

"Thank you, Howard." Carl's shoulders relaxed. He lost his look of incipient werewolfhood, and went away.

The dinner. When it was over, Howard could think of eating again. He was almost beginning to get his appetite back even now. He had lost twenty-five pounds in his neurotic fits, and his clothes hung on him. After he left here he would never have to wear a suit and tie again. Golf shirts. He would wear golf shirts and khakis for the rest of his days, and put the weight back on, and have little titties, just like his father-in-law, and he would make love to Ophelia every morning and every night.

Howard had no sooner got the safe open and begun sorting through its contents than Jared Baines came barging into the office. Baines. The first time they met, Howard had found his manners annoying, and even felt a twinge of pity for the Porcpharm employees whom he would be leaving behind to work under the man. Baines did not improve upon acquaintance; after the deal with Supra Labs was struck he grew much worse. What did he want now? To triumph over Howard, apparently.

"So, Howard," said Baines. "In forty-eight hours the responsibilities of this place will be lifted from your weary shoulders."

"Yes, that's true," said Howard. "Would you like some coffee?"

Jared Baines laughed scornfully. "Thank you, no," he said. "Even in Hackensack, we've heard about your coffee."

"Oh, I . . . I didn't mean . . ."

"Forty-eight hours. Looking forward to it? What's the first thing you're going to do?"

"Ophelia and I are planning to travel. It's been a long time since we had some time together away from the children, and we thought . . ."

"Then on Monday we'll clear out the deadwood. Twenty percent across the board. I must tell you, Howard, I'm really looking forward to taking over the helm here. Turning Porcpharm into a big revenue generator for Supraordinate Laboratories will be the most exciting challenge of my corporate career. To date, that is."

"Yes," said Howard. It seemed to be the only thing left to say.

"I think I can tell you now, without revealing anything damaging to our agreement, that if it weren't for hivostatin, your company wouldn't have been interesting to Supra Labs at all."

"No?" said Howard. Actually he knew this already.

"No, and particularly not after the Wankemol poisoning scare. How far did sales drop off after that? Seventy-five percent?"

"Sixty," Howard said absently.

"But the contract offers from those third world governments made a deal too sweet to turn down." He sighed comfortably, and sat down uninvited in one of Howard's chairs.

Bang! The door burst open. The umbrella stand fell over.

Ophelia stood in the doorway, her hair flying, her eyes wild. He hadn't seen her this way since the time that she and Carl—

"Howard."

"Ophelia! My dear. What brings you—"

"Howard, what have you and Carl been doing?"

"I don't know what you mean."

"Yes you do, Howard."

"Well, but, it was only . . ."

"I can't allow this to continue."

"It's only for two more days. After the merger becomes final—"

"Is there some problem?" said Baines. Ophelia turned and stared at him.

"No, no," Howard said. "A family matter. Ophelia, please, can't you see that Jared, here, doesn't need to share in our . . ."

"After the merger becomes final, what?" said Baines.

There was a beat of silence, and then Howard and Ophelia both spoke together. Howard said, "Why then, we'll decide where to travel," and Ophelia said, "Then Howard will tell you that hivostatin is teratogenic."

"Teratogenic?" said Baines, the color draining from his face. "Does that mean what I think it does?"

"Yes," Ophelia said. "It causes birth defects. The bodies of damaged infant apes were found buried on the grounds here, the results of experiments."

"How damaged were they?" said Baines.

"Severely," said Ophelia. "No arms. No legs."

Well, thought Howard, *this foolish woman has ruined both our futures.*

"Why, Howard?" she said. "Knowing this, why did you go ahead and manufacture it? Running the factory all day and all night to produce this—this criminally harmful drug."

Ruined. Baines would call off the merger, and they would all go down the drain along with Porcpharm. He began to feel sick. Maybe he was poisoned. So what? It was all over now.

But instead of shouting or demanding to tear up the contract, Jared Baines stood very still and stroked his chin, a chess player contemplating an unexpected move by his opponent.

"Hope you don't mind if I use your phone," he said at last. Howard said nothing, and Ophelia, still raging, watched the two of them in silence.

Baines dialed an area code and a number. "Manny," he said. "Jared Baines here. I need freight transportation from Princeton, New Jersey, to Kinshasa.

"It's in Zaire. It's the capital of Zaire. Yes, there's an airport, we could ship by air, but there's a lot of product and I'd sooner put it on a freighter, maybe in Port Newark or Philadelphia. Kinshasa has deep-water port facilities, I'm almost certain. The Congo is navigable pretty far upriver.

"Okay, good. Also the trucks to get it out of here, preferably tonight. Call me at this number." He repeated Howard's office phone number. "I want to hear from you in fifteen minutes." He hung up.

"You can't do this," said Ophelia. "You have no authority."

"Howard will give me all the authority I need. Won't you, Howard? I might point out to you that we have to move very quickly on this."

"But, you can't!" she said. Howard thought, *She really is very beautiful when she's angry.*

Baines looked at her, holding her gaze, as though to overpower her with the force of his corporate mojo. He said, "My dear, there's nothing illegal in any of it."

"I'm not sure that's true," she said.

"What is it that bothers you?" he said. "Gays don't have babies."

"AIDS in Africa is a heterosexual problem," she said. "The government of Zaire plans to distribute hivostatin to everyone in the country who is sexually active. That's the entire population between the ages of thirteen and eighty, excluding Roman Catholic priests and nuns."

He shrugged. "It isn't as though we were shipping the stuff to Bergen County," he said. "Africans don't sue."

"Mr. Baines," she said, "if you send hivostatin to Zaire, thousands of babies will be born next year without any arms or legs." He shrugged. She rounded on Howard. "Aren't you going to do anything?" she said. "Aren't you going to say anything?" Her skin was white all around the nostrils.

"Ophelia," he said to her, "dearest, you must realize that I meant to release the true results of those tests as soon as the merger went through."

"Did you?" she said. "Why didn't you stop its manufacture?" So that Supra Labs wouldn't be tipped off. That was why. He couldn't tell her that in front of Jared, though.

When he didn't answer her, she left, slamming the door behind her. Maybe she had a point after all.

"I wish you would hold off on this shipment you're proposing, Jared," Howard said. "Ophelia's right, you know; it's wrong to distribute this drug before tests are complete."

"I don't know what you people are whining about," said Baines. "The problem is all taken care of."

"No," Howard said. "Suppose the UN finds out. Maybe the World Court will sue." He really ought to talk about this with the company lawyers. He should have discussed it with them long ago. What could he have been thinking of? No telling what might happen now.

Baines sighed. "By the time the World Court gets its ass in gear, Porcineau Pharmaceuticals will be an independent company again and in chapter eleven bankruptcy proceedings. There'll be nothing to sue. Trust me. It's a no-lose situation. Take the money and run, is my advice."

Howard said, "Jared, I can still announce the failure of tests on the drug."

"Well, Howard, I guess the time has come to point out to you what happens in this great republic of ours to people who conspire to defraud."

"What do you mean?" said Howard, feeling sicker.

"I mean you're going to take the money and leave all this to me. If you don't, if you open your mouth about this to anybody, you'll go to prison, where you can have a look at the AIDS problem firsthand, if you take my meaning. Remember, it wasn't my idea to bury your little birth defects out on the grounds."

Ophelia Strass did not rush out to her car and drive home after confronting Howard. She wanted to, but there was the dinner to get through, her last gesture toward the doomed employees of Porcineau Pharmaceuticals. Mother would be there. It was necessary for Ophelia to show up and smile serenely, and conceal her revulsion at the plateful of dead chicken flesh they would give her.

She went into the ladies' room and splashed water on her face. In her mind she saw the African children from the villages where she had worked with the Peace Corps, giggling, half naked, full of life. She tried to imagine their lives without arms and legs.

She patted her face with a brown, medicinal-smelling paper towel, renewed her lipstick, and went out into the hall, turning in the direction of the atrium. If she had only kept control of her Porcpharm shares! Howard didn't have good sense. Always a mistake to put power in the hands of such people. In their youth, she had mistaken Howard's calm demeanor for wisdom and maturity. She envied him the ability to bridle his passions. At last the truth dawned on her: He had no passions to bridle. The man was an empty shell.

Kevin Mandelbaum was in Nick Magaracz's office, trying to explain the fresh idea he had for questioning Jewel the monkey. He looked up as Ophelia Strass came striding down the hall, silhouetted against the light of the farther corridor, her coat flying. She stopped abruptly at the door to the office when she saw Nick sitting at his desk.

"How are you?" she said. "Are you all right?"

"I'm okay," he said. "Thanks for the flowers."

Then she seemed to notice Kevin. He couldn't keep himself from staring at her; something about her struck him as enormously attractive. "I'm sorry," she said. "I'm interrupting you."

"Not at all," said Kevin.

Magaracz introduced them. "Ophelia Strass, this is Kevin Mandelbaum. He's with New Life Systems."

"How do you do?" she said. She offered him her hand, firm and warm, a hand that could handle a horse or a lot of money. "What is New Life Systems?" she said.

"I'm a social worker," he said. "My services are contracted out to employees of Porcineau Pharmaceuticals —and—and their families, as a benefit."

She seemed strangely interested. Maybe even the wife of arch capitalist Howie Strass needed counseling from time to time. Or was she being polite? How lovely she was.

"I was telling Kevin he ought to join COGPAR," said Magaracz. "He's a great believer in animal rights."

She said, "Really? I suppose we could use some men. They could, I mean." She sounded unsure of her own affiliation with the group; Kevin pointed this out to her, and with a rueful little smile she said, "You're very perceptive. I bet you're very good at your work."

Kevin gave her one of his cards. "If you find that you need counseling about anything, please feel free to give me a call, or come by the office," he said.

"I may do that," she said. "I'm in a situation right now where I need all the help I can get."

Was she serious? Was he? He smiled. "I'm free right now," he said. "My office is right down the hall, if you . . ."

"What time is it?" she said.

"Six twenty-five."

"Oh, my God, the dinner. Are you going, Kevin?"

"No," he said. "Strictly speaking, I'm not a Porcpharm employee. Our services are contracted—"

"Mother will be here any minute," she said, biting her lip. "Please excuse me. Perhaps I'll have a chance to talk to you afterwards. Will you be here?"

"Certainly."

"Good. Maybe I'll see you then." She rushed off down the hall.

"Well, whaddeya know," said Magaracz.

"Isn't she something?" said Kevin. "Is she really Howard's wife?"

" 'Fraid so," said Magaracz. "And not only that."

"What?"

"She's one of my chief murder suspects."

Nineteen

In the Porcpharm cafeteria kitchen, security guards eyed the caterers mercilessly. Thanks to Hester's tireless efforts among her publishing friends, the story of Porcpharm's recent troubles had made the papers only obliquely, as a series of apparently unrelated obituary notices. Thus it was that Iz Silverstein had no idea that he was being asked to cater an affair where everyone was expecting to be poisoned.

"How come they don't want us to set the fruit cup on the tables, like we always do?" whined the caterer's assistant.

"Beats the hell out of me," said Silverstein. "They just said nothing to eat or drink on the tables until everyone was seated." One of the security men was fishing pineapple bits out of the salad and eating them. "Quit that," said Silverstein. "What are you guys doing out here, anyway? Why don't you get out from under our feet and let us work?"

"Orders from Mr. Strass," the man said. "Hey! What's that stuff you're putting on the fruit?"

"Bitters," Silverstein replied. "It's a house recipe. What's it to you?"

The security guard sniffed the bottle. "Sure it ain't poison?"

The caterer took the bottle and had a swig. He smacked his lips with a grin at the security guard. "Haah!" he breathed. "Delicious!" The bitters stained his teeth. The security guard backed away. "This place is a zoo," Silverstein muttered. "Next year they can get somebody else to do the dinner."

"It doesn't seem right," his assistant grumbled. "Cops all over the kitchen. No fruit cup on the tables." A bevy of uniformed waitresses collected the fruit cups and paraded into the atrium to deliver them to the waiting diners.

In that forest of philodendron and Benjamin fig where the tables were set for dinner, the employees who were required to attend the awards ceremony were showing signs of stress and tension. Many were smoking, in direct contravention of the company rule (or was it a federal rule?) that smoking was forbidden in the atrium. Others were shredding their paper napkins, or building little structures out of their knives and forks. Now and then one of them could be heard cracking his knuckles.

Nobody knew for certain which of them would lose their jobs on Monday when the takeover by Supraordinate Laboratories became final. Colleagues withdrew from one another, fearing the contagion of failure. Subordinates clammed up in the presence of supervisors, having heard that the hit list had been compiled, fearing the boss had put them on it, knowing the boss could be on it too. Pointless to cultivate the goodwill of a person who could be powerless the day after tomorrow, or who might have betrayed you already.

Then, too, there was the added strain of poison fears. It was generally known now that the poisoner was real, and was among them. It was not known who would be next. So the Porcpharm employees sat uneasily, eight to a table, dressed for success, fearing to speak, pretending to eat and drink.

There was wine at the dinner, both red and white. The customary cash bar was not in evidence. Two weeks before the affair Howard had been forced to entertain a delegation of Mothers Against Drunk Driving, of which Mary Mavis, his secretary, had been a member ever since her son was run over and killed by drunken teenagers. The Mothers had spoken to Howard sternly about the practice of the cash bar. They pointed out to him that the availability of so much alcohol so far from public transportation could result in tragedy, followed by lawsuits and criminal actions. Howard capitulated. Only wine was served, and not very much of that.

Nevertheless, Margaret Gagne appeared somehow to be getting snockered. Magaracz, seated next to her at the head table, observed her as the hooded eyes grew more and more hooded and the head was carried at a more and more artificially dignified angle.

They had put him between the biochemist and Hester Porcineau, too far from Howie, really, to grab his food away, even if by some phenomenon of extrasensory perception he were able to detect that it was poisoned. Magaracz assumed that what he was really there for was to make the CEO feel safe.

I'm a rabbit's foot, he said to himself. "Maybe I should stand behind your chair," he had suggested to Howard, "like a secret service man." But Big Howie had rejected this suggestion, saying it would make the whole arrangement too conspicuous, as if he didn't stick out now in his number-two suit with the cockleburs still clinging to it from his morning walk in the woods.

"How is your wife?" Hester said to him, picking a cocklebur from his right sleeve. "You should have brought her."

"Yeah, well," said Magaracz. They had discussed it; she kind of wanted to come, but he wouldn't let her, on account of she might get poisoned.

Hester turned to the man on her right, one of the geriatric board members who had left their haunts in Palm Springs to put in an appearance at this shindig, and engaged him in chitchat about the weather. As Magaracz sat staring moodily into his fruit cup it struck him suddenly that he was bored with this case. He had never been bored with a case before, not even in his earliest private-dick days, when he supported himself and Ethel by peeping at your ordinary run-of-the-mill adulterers.

At least with adultery there was always a little of the old hot-cha-cha. But this—! One guy gets killed, and then another guy gets killed, and then another. You want to talk tedious. He was hoping to get some clues or something from Ophelia when she showed up in his office; he was sure she was upset and willing to talk;

evidently, though, what she really wanted was to be social-worked. A dull business.

Most boring of all was getting poisoned himself. Bodily injury had never appealed to Magaracz, not even when he was nineteen. He wasn't up for it. Furthermore, he feared that the poisoning attack might have damaged his mind, which such as it was was still his stock in trade. Things were still turning into other things as he watched and Nick Magaracz did not feel like his old self.

Maybe he would quit.

"I know something you don't know, Mr. Detective," said Margaret Gagne. Her water glass was half-full of vodka. God knows where she was getting it, the old hip flask in the pocketbook, maybe. He could smell what it was; he could see its effect on her. Maybe there was somebody at the table who thought it was water. Nick Magaracz was not fooled.

She put her hand over his hand. Her skin was dry and rough, chemicals probably, or frequent washing. "I know a secret," she breathed at him. "I think I'll tell it to you now." He would quit. After this stupid dinner he would tell Howie to get another detective.

He patted her hand. "You would be smart to tell me everything you know," he said, "considering what happened to Munsen and Pollert. If you haven't any secrets, then it's no longer worth anyone's while to kill you to keep you quiet. Know what I'm saying?"

Nobody else at the table seemed to be listening to their conversation. Caroline Gables was gushing at Jared Baines about the possibilities of hivostatin. "Of course, I understand that hivostatin is a wonderful resource and a tremendous boon to world health." Baines appeared to be paying attention. Hettie was jawing at J. Potter Pitterpatter or whatever his name was about the greenhouse effect. Pitterpatter was dozing. Ophelia was charming the other old board member. Howard was occupied with waving and smiling at his cronies and subordinates, waving the same well-manicured hands that had mixed the very coffee that put Magaracz in Princeton Medical Center. Carl Gables was not in his place; presumably he had gone to the men's room.

They might as well have been alone. "Is this about the burials in the golf course?" Magaracz guessed.

"No," said Margaret Gagne. "I know nothing about any burials. No, it's this." She leaned closer. All at once Magaracz was no longer bored. In the movies, he realized, this would be the moment when a handgun with a silencer would come poking through the window and put an end to the doctor's confidences. There were no windows here in the atrium. Nick Magaracz cast a glance at every bush and doorway. It looked safe.

"Fire away," he said.

"You were asking me the other day about Carl Gables's injuries," Dr. Gagne said in a low voice.

"Yes," said Magaracz. "What's the story?"

"The story, as you put it, is that I probably saved the man's life."

Caroline Gables at the other end of the table was urging a humanitarian project on Jared Baines. "I wonder whether you've considered—have you thought about giving the drug away?" she asked him.

"Giving it away?" said Baines, seemingly stupefied.

"He was being beaten," Magaracz prompted. "With a stick."

"Beaten, with a stick, by none other than the lovely

Ophelia Porcineau Strass. I pulled her off him, or she would have killed him for certain.''

Magaracz had trouble imagining it. "Why would she do that?"

"Mr. Magaracz, I assumed that he was, as they say, trying to force his attentions on her. He was bare-assed. Maybe he was taking a bath, but the executive showers are in another wing of the building. He was quite a sight." She narrowed her eyes, and leaned even closer. "I've never seen so much hair on a human being."

"Yes, give it away," said the hairy one's wife. "Something on the order of ivermectin, the drug that prevents river blindness in Africa. I understand that Merck is making it available for free to the affected countries."

Baines stroked his chin, a granite monument of blue stubble. Evidently he hadn't heard about ivermectin. "Why would they . . ."

"Goodwill," said Caroline Gibbons. "Wonderful public relations. It was a cover story for the *New York Times Magazine.*"

"Goodwill," Baines mouthed, as though the words had an unfamiliar taste.

"Long-term goodwill is worth a lot," Caroline insisted.

Magaracz whispered, "What shape was Ophelia in at this point? Was she undressed?"

"Well, now, let me—No, hardly a hair out of place. I guess he never got a chance to touch her. She was mad, though. I heard him screaming and I came in, and she had him down, hitting him. It was all I could do to make her stop, and get the animals back in their cages, and all that.''

A scene from hell, thought Magaracz. "So what did she say to you about all this?"

"Nothing, but she never speaks to me anyway. I'm that scarlet woman who tried to break up her happy home. Or did you know that?" Magaracz, almost surprised, searched her face for traces of the irresistible Fleur du Mal. Then he looked at Ophelia, laughing politely at one of old Potterputter's even older jokes, her slim hand on his arm. Beating a man with a stick? Not a mark on her, either; he must have just lain there and taken it. Carl Gables slipped back into his seat, far enough away from his sister-in-law, the detective was happy to see, so that she could not reach him, should she have a sudden murderous impulse to prong him with a dinner fork.

"I don't know why," said Magaracz to Dr. Gagne, "but I kind of thought it was you that beat up our boy there."

"No, Mr. Magaracz, outraged innocence—Hah! Hah!—isn't my style." The mere idea was enough to start her on a fit of coughing. She groped for a cigarette.

Jared Baines, after some thought, had framed a reply to Caroline's altruistic suggestion. "Mrs. Gables," he said with a little laugh, "I have to make Porcpharm generate revenues within the year. Supra Labs insists on a reasonable return on its investment." Again he chuckled. "Goodwill," he said: "After the Wankemol poisonings? Porcpharm's goodwill is a joke. A national joke."

Hester dropped her dinner napkin and as she bent to pick it up gave a little grunt.

"You know, Howard," she said, "You still have

gravy stains between the tiles on this floor from the other dinner."

Howard looked blank. "What gravy stains? What other dinner? We held this at the fire hall last year, Mother Porcineau, and before that at the Hyatt."

"Hah! Hah!" barked Margaret Gagne, and took a deep drag on her forbidden and malodorous cigarette. "That's no gravy stain, honey, that's all that's left of poor old Artie Munsen."

Everyone at the table turned to stare at her, appalled.

Ophelia said, "Howard. This isn't where that man— Is it?"

"I'll have to speak to the cleaning staff," Howard mumbled, rubbing his head.

After that, nobody at the table ate anything at all. Finally the dessert came.

Howard Strass stood up and tinked his spoon on a glass. The assembled company, not particularly relaxed to start with, came tautly to attention. Howard drew breath to speak.

Suddenly all eyes flew to the main lobby entrance behind him. Two police officers, a man and a woman, had appeared in the doorway. They were speaking with a uniformed security man, who pointed toward the head table. The officers approached purposefully.

"Dr. Margaret Gagne?" the policewoman inquired.

"I am Dr. Gagne," the biochemist said, a fresh drink of "water" poised before her lips.

"I'll have to ask you to come with me. I have a warrant for your arrest for the murder of Alfred Munsen."

As the policewoman produced a pair of handcuffs,

Dr. Gagne took a swig. Then she dropped like a captured spy with her face in the peach melba.

Right after that came the screaming, the hysterical
vomiting, and the surreptitious depositing of food from
mouths back onto plates as the other diners realized
that someone had actually been poisoned. Magaracz
could have sworn that none of them had touched a
bite, and yet here came all this half-chewed food.

Howard jumped up shouting, "Oh my God, not Margaret," and bounded over to her, feeling in his pockets.
He pushed the police aside and sniffed at Dr. Gagne's
lips. "Bitter almonds," he said. From his breast pocket
he drew a small handful of glass capsules and crushed
them into his handkerchief.

"What are you doing?" the policeman said.

"This is amyl nitrate," Howard said, holding the
handkerchief to Dr. Gagne's face. "We make it here at
Porcpharm. I just happened to be carrying it. It's
... ah ... it's antidotal in potassium cyanide poisoning."

Jared Baines appeared at Howard's elbow. "Cyanide!" he said. He began picking up drinking glasses,
cups, and tableware, sniffing them, turning them
around in his hands.

"You probably shouldn't be doing that," Nick Magaracz said to him. "I believe this is a crime scene, and
those things might be evidence."

"Please don't touch anything, sir," the police officer
agreed.

"Who are you?" said Jared Baines, with a stony
stare at Magaracz.

"That's Nick Magaracz, Jared," Howard said, without looking up. He was crushing more perles into his
handkerchief. "He works for me. Security."

"Is this what you Princeton people call security?" said Baines, with a gesture at the unconscious bio-chemist.

"Not me," said Magaracz. "I'm a Trenton person."

"If you want me for anything," said Baines to the police officers, "have me paged. I'll be in the building. I'm Jared Baines."

"Where can you be reached later, sir?" the police-man murmured.

"I'm at the Hyatt," said Baines, and disappeared into the depths of the west wing.

Twenty

T hat was the end of the dinner; they never gave out the awards.

But all the while that these events were taking place, busy hands were piling crates by the doors of the loading bays in the rear of the west wing of Porcineau Pharmaceuticals. As the rescue squad ambulance bore Margaret Gagne away into the Central Jersey night—lights flashing, siren howling—a dark unmarked truck turned into the driveway labeled "shipping" and made its quiet way to those very loading bays.

Operation Hivodump, as Jared Baines called it in his mind, was under way.

The trick was going to be getting the product outside the continental limits before any inconvenient injunctions could be issued. But Jared Baines had the problem in hand. He had not climbed to the upper rungs of the corporate ladder by being indecisive or misreading corporate goals and intentions; by this swift stroke he would maximize in dollar terms the only real asset that Porcpharm still had—the third world's belief in the power of hivostatin—and thus win the praise and approval of his masters at Supra Labs.

Load up the trucks, run for the docks, worry about telling a straight story later. As the earliest of the trucks backed up to the loading dock, Baines stood waiting, arms folded across his chest. He would give the trucker a pep talk, maybe promise him a bonus if he could get the shipment to Port Newark before the *Queen of Nigeria* sailed. Then back to his office to goose Howard into getting his garbage out of there.

It was nine o'clock. Both east and west wings of the building were almost empty of people. Porcpharm's security staff had moved quickly to block the exits from the atrium after Dr. Gagne's unfortunate episode, leaving the main door that led into the front lobby for the homicide police to cover. There they took names and addresses, and told people they could go, but not to go very far.

This was, of course, ridiculous. Many of the Porcpharm employees commuted unimaginable distances at high speed in their Audis and BMWs, from Long Island, Toms River, South Philadelphia. They were forced to leave town—Greater Princeton, that is—to go home, and this they did, still hungry for the most part, or they went to the Fox, as the local watering hole was called, there to denounce this latest manifestation of Howard's incompetence, and to drink, and maybe to eat something, and then to drive back to their dwellings.

Magaracz considered tagging along to the Fox for a quick drink. If he kept his ears open he might get a lead. But, no, he had a lead, two important clues in fact, and for a change both of them pointed in the same direction.

Ophelia Strass.

Where was she? Had she left with the other Porcineau women? Or had she kept her appointment with young Kevin Mandelbaum? Howard was still in the building someplace. He had told Magaracz to come to his office later, murmuring this request as the rescue squad trundled the gurney carrying Margaret Gagne down the front ramp. She was still alive, Magaracz figured, since the rescue squad hadn't covered her face, but her breathing was very shallow and faint.

"How much later?" said Magaracz. He really wanted to go home.

"Fifteen minutes," Howie said. "I need to talk to you about all this." Revelations! Revelations were coming at last! Howie was going to open up! Magaracz gave a brief statement to the cops, mostly explaining how he had just been sitting there the whole time, doing nothing, but how he was actually on the case.

"Why was Dr. Gagne being arrested?" Nick asked them.

"For the murder of Arthur Munsen," said the policewoman.

"No kidding," said Magaracz. "Then who poisoned her?"

"She did it herself," the policeman said. "We see it

all the time. Why do you think we take people's ties and shoelaces in the lockup?"

"What makes them think she killed Munsen?" Magaracz asked.

"He left a letter with his lawyer, to be opened in case of his death. It seems she threatened to kill him."

A lover's quarrel. She couldn't have meant it. If she did, though, how would it fit into everything else?

Fleur du Mal, the spider woman. *She killed the men she loved.* Or tried to; had it been Margaret who took all those shots at Howard? She could have faked the tests when he asked the lab to check for poison.

But somehow it didn't fit. Magaracz was growing more and more certain that the real killer was none other than Ophelia herself.

Still, Margaret was a possibility. Magaracz called Princeton Medical Center to find out how she was doing. He was able to speak with Dr. Dey, the same guy who had treated him for poisoning.

"Your friend is lucky," the doctor said. "We think she's going to make it. She seems to have ingested potassium cyanide somehow."

"Not like what I had," said Magaracz.

"No, nothing at all. If you had taken the dose of cyanide that she did, you would be dead. But Dr. Gagne—I only tell you this because I know you're working on the case, and that you'll keep it in confidence—Dr. Gagne is a chronic alcoholic. She suffers from alcoholic gastritis."

Magaracz was not surprised to hear this, but he did wonder what it had to do with anything.

"It's a curious phenomenon of alcoholic gastritis that it protects a patient to a certain extent from the effects of poisoning by cyanide salts. You see, the rapidity with which the salts cause death upon ingestion depends on the amount of hydrochloric acid present at the time the salt was swallowed. This affects the quantity of hydrogen cyanide which is then liberated and absorbed by the gastric mucosa."

"Right," said Magaracz. So she was still alive because she was a drunk. Well, it was something to think about. They said the same thing about Uncle Stash the time he fell down the cellar stairs.

"Then, too," said the doctor, "the prompt administration of amyl nitrate was extremely beneficial. I wonder how Mr. Strass happened to have it on his person."

"He was expecting trouble," said Magaracz. *After all,* he thought, *he knows his own wife best.* "How soon can she talk to somebody?" he asked the doctor.

"You and the police both want to know that," said Dr. Dey. "I cannot tell. Certainly not tonight. She has not yet regained consciousness."

It struck him that he'd better go see Howie. The way this case was going Ophelia was probably up there right now feeding him poison.

In fact, Ophelia was wandering the maze-like halls, thinking apocalyptic thoughts. *It's the end for me and Howard.* Fifteen years out the window. She would have to divorce him for philosophical incompatibility. Were there such grounds as that in New Jersey? Tomorrow she would talk to a lawyer. Poisoning fetuses. It was too much. No, it was the end.

She felt too deeply upset to get behind the wheel of a car. Remembering her tentative appointment with the social worker, she had set out to keep it.

For a while she moved without plan through the

dimly-lit halls, hoping to come upon his office by in-
stinct. She walked very fast, stretching her legs out.
Exercise in itself was helpful; her head began to clear.

As she came around the next corner she saw the
menacing bulk of a man approaching.

"Excuse me," the man called.

It was too late to avoid him. "Yes?" she said. He was
dressed as a cowboy or a sheep farmer and smelled
faintly of machine oil. His ham-like hands gripped a
clipboard with papers on it, yellow, white, and pink.
His fingernails were filthy.

"Can you tell me where Jared Baines's office is?" he
said. "I need him to sign these papers and I can't find
his office. This place is real easy to get lost in."

She said, "It's back that way," and then she realized
that she was lost herself. The building was constructed
with the corridors at odd angles to one another. The
numbering of the rooms was not in logical sequence.
"We need a map," she said.

There was one on the corridor wall by the corner of
the building. A yellow dot told them, "You are here."
She found Howard's office on the map for the man;
presumably Jared Baines would occupy that office
now. He hoofed it off in the right direction, the heels
of his cowboy boots going *thok, thok* on the vinyl tile.

Kevin Mandelbaum's card had his room number
scrawled on the back. It was on another floor after all.
If the room numbers corresponded from one floor to
the next, his office would be down the stairs, around
the corner, and two corridors farther on.

She found it easily. The light was on, the door was
open, and the social worker was brewing herb tea.

"I'm so glad you're here," she said. "This is the most
god-awful mess."

Twenty-one

Magaracz went up the stairs as fast as he could without getting out of breath and charged into Howie's fancy executive office, knocking over the umbrella stand. Howie, Jared Baines, and Carl Gables were all standing around the big mahogany desk looking vaguely guilty, like stray dogs around a garbage can. In the middle of the desk was a brown paper bag, the top folded over twice, a gravy stain slowly spreading near the bottom. A smell of Chinese food filled the office. Magaracz's worst fears were confirmed.

He stared pointedly at the bag. "Did Ophelia bring you this food?" he said. "I'd think twice before I ate it, if I were you, Howie."

Howard said, "Why, no. What makes you ask?"

"I dunno," said Magaracz. What was he thinking of? He felt confused. The effects of his poisoning were creeping back again.

A cowboy appeared with a clipboard full of papers. Jared Baines said, "What, are you still here?"

"I need your signature on this shipping authorization form, Mr. Baines," said the cowboy impassively. "I can't leave without it, as I told you before."

"All right, then, here," said Baines, and scrawled his signature across four separate copies. "Now get going."

"You need to keep the second copy," said the cowboy. *Bureaucrats,* thought Magaracz. *Bureaucrats in every walk of life.* Baines took the yellow copy and the cowboy left.

With a sigh of relief Baines pulled out Howard's contour swivel desk chair and sat in it. "I'm glad you're here, Carl," he said to Gables. "This will save you the trouble of coming in next week. We're letting you go."

"I was expecting that, Jared," said Gables.

"Yes, I know you were. I thought I'd do you a favor and tell you now. Give you a chance to clean your desk out, say good-bye to any of the animals you might be particularly fond of, all that good stuff." He took his shoes off and stretched his feet out on the desk. His socks were black. His feet did not smell of sandalwood.

"Thank you very much," said Gables, but somehow he didn't really sound grateful. "Speaking of cleaning, Howard, do you think you could let me have that photograph that we left in your safe? Just as a memento."

"It's on my desk," said Howard, pointing to a small manila interoffice envelope, the kind with the holes, resting on top of a pile of papers.

Something showing through one of the holes, a glimpse of something hairy, caused Magaracz to wake up a little. This could be important. "Mind if I see that?" he said, grabbing the envelope before Gables could get to it.

Carl Gables and Howie Strass seemed momentarily paralyzed. They stood there like guys with their feet in cement. What was the big deal? Magaracz knew the worst that could be in it.

"What's that?" demanded Jared Baines.

Magaracz looked at the manila envelope. "My guess is, it's a picture of deformed baby apes," he said. "But I'm going to have to keep it. It's evidence; I need it for the investigation." He slipped it out of the envelope and had a cautious look.

It wasn't what he thought. Instead, it was a black-and-white Polaroid snapshot of Carl Gables and Jewel.

Oddly enough, they seemed an attractive couple. Magaracz had seen blue movies where the participants seemed to be less well-matched. The approach they were using was fairly primitive, but then, what did you expect? She was an ape. Bemused, he put the photograph back in the envelope. Then he thought, *I bet this is another hallucination.*

"We'll just take care of that right now," said Jared Baines. Springing to his feet, he seized the manila envelope. "Evidence, my ass. You people thought you could use this to back out of the merger with Supraordinate Laboratories, didn't you?" He took out a cigarette lighter and set fire to it. "I'll show you what I think of your pathetic plan." While they watched he dangled the burning envelope over the free-form ceramic ashtray and dropped it just in time to keep from burning his fingers. The last ashes crisped and curled.

"Now all of you people shut up and go away," he said. "This is my office now and I have work to do. You're fired, by the way, Nick, you don't work for this company anymore. That leaves two hundred ninety-six more to go. Give your key card to the guard on your way out."

Fired. The word reverberated in Magaracz's head as in a large, empty auditorium. *This is the end of the day for me,* he thought. *The end.* He was completely wiped out. Days in the hospital, he couldn't remember how many, a gruelling schedule on his first day out, and now this strange insidious betrayal by his own five senses. Stupefaction was creeping over him like a fog.

He had to go home. But there was something he had come up here for—to save Howard—

As if from a great distance he heard Howard say, "I'll take my supper with me, if you don't mind."

"But I do," said Baines. "I mind if you take your goddam supper with you. I tell you what, I think I'll eat it myself. We paid you plenty for this company; go buy yourself another goddam supper."

He closed the door on their backs.

Nick Magaracz returned to his office one last time to pick up his coat and his "World's Greatest Husband" mug. A couple of felt-tip pens and a steno notebook went into his pockets as well. On his way out through the rat-maze of halls he noticed a light under Kevin Mandelbaum's door and heard the soft desperate sounds of a woman weeping.

Kevin Mandelbaum found that he was completely be-sotted with this woman who was crying on his desk blotter. He wanted to hold her and stroke her hair. It would feel, he knew, kind of electric and crispy. Her shoulder blades were so thin. She was the most elegant woman he had ever seen in person.

He gave her the box of Kleenex, and offered her tea. "I have three kinds," he said, "Red Zinger, orange pekoe, and chamomile." She chose chamomile.

"You need to talk," he told her. "Tell me what's bothering you."

"It's Howard," she said. "He has done the most terrible things. If I had known he could do such things I never would have married him. It's as though he were a stranger. Fifteen years with a stranger. I don't know what to do."

"When you say terrible things, you mean . . ." he prompted. Howard! Howard was the killer! Was Magaracz still here? Should he call the police? But, no; this was a professional confidence.

"I've never sought counseling before," she said. "But this is such a mess."

"Has he tried to harm you?"

"Harm me?" She looked up at him and wiped her nose. Her eyes were so . . . limpid. That was the word, limpid. And sublime. He could drown in them.

"Not physically," she said, "but who knows? A stranger is a stranger. He might do anything. I have no way of knowing what he might do." She pulled herself together, smoothed her skirt, took a fresh piece of Kleenex, and tended to her face. "We have two daughters," she said.

"I see," he murmured encouragingly, although he really didn't.

"And yet, I'm afraid I'm going to have to leave him. I'm so sorry for what this will do to them, but what else can I do?"

"I don't know," he said. "Let's explore that." She
was leaving Howard. Maybe Kevin had a chance with
her. Had her husband tried to kill her? Was she all
right? Did he dare to take her hand? He took her hand.
Then he patted it, trying to seem fatherly, a neat trick
if he could do it, seeing that she was a good ten years
older.

She took her hand back, using it to push a lock of
hair behind her ear. "The problem with Howard is
. . . Are you sure this conversation is confidential?"

"Confidential between client and counselor."

"You could never be forced to repeat it in court?"

"No," he said.

"Because it may come to that. Howard may have to
go to jail."

"I can never be forced to repeat anything you tell
me in court," he said. He hoped that was right.

"Then I'll tell you what Howard has done," she said.

Nick Magaracz did not surrender his key card to the
security guard.

It wasn't that he was planning with his usual dogged
persistence to track the case to its end. The quality of
dogged persistence seemed to have departed from
him, at least for the moment, and he wanted nothing
more than to say good-bye to this stupid, dangerous
case and go home to Ethel. She did say lasagna. Maybe
some was left.

With that in mind—the picture of Ethel's incompa-
rable homemade tomato sauce, spicy hot Italian sausage, lean, tender ground beef, succulent pasta, warm,
yielding ricotta, mozzarella clinging to fork and plate
in mouth-watering strings—he could almost smell it—

with that thought driving him, Nick Magaracz completely forgot to give his key card to the security guard
on the way out. It was not a conscious decision. But it
was a good thing, because on his way to the parking lot
he saw something that put him back on the crime-
busting trail.

What he saw was a brand-new van of the sort that
cost twice as much as Nick and Ethel had paid for their
little Yardville home. It was parked on the sidewalk by
the east wing, next to a well with concrete steps leading down to a dark doorway. The side door of the van
was open, and the dome light was on, revealing the
voluptuous interior. Here was a travel vehicle of great
luxury, in which a man might drive enormous distances, to Florida, to California, to Mexico, even, in
total comfort, and take his sweetie with him, espe-
cially if his sweetie was one that required the bars on
the windows with which this elegant vehicle seemed to
have been fitted up.

In a flash Magaracz understood the series of events
that had landed Gables in the hospital: Ophelia, sneak-
ing into the building in her chic black burglar suit,
looking for maltreated animals, finding her brother-in-
law engaged in gross misconduct, snapping the picture, losing her temper, beating him. This was a
woman who did not hesitate to resort to violence in
defense of abused animals.

Afterwards, had she told sister Caroline? Probably
not. There were many families where this kind of information was never exchanged. To talk would be considered hurtful and destructive.

Magaracz wondered what the monkey was doing
while Ophelia was working her sweetie over with a big

stick. Eating a candy bar, probably. One thing puzzled
him.

What made Howard keep the picture?

Of course. To blackmail his brother-in-law into help-
ing him cover up the birth defects. Family secrets.

So Howard was blackmailing Carl.

Naturally Carl tried to kill him.

Like dominoes the elements of the case fell into
place in Magaracz's revitalized mind, one by one,
click, click, until everything was revealed. Who would
be the next victim?

Or did anyone have to be next? The incriminating
picture had been destroyed. On the other hand, three
living people other than Gables had seen it. *Including
me,* he thought.

It was starting to rain. Cold drops fell on his face.
What am I doing? he said to himself. *The killer is
getting away.*

Magaracz looked down the dark stairway, weighing
his options. *I can stand here and confront him when
they try to get in the van,* he thought. In his mind they
appeared before him: Carl Gables and Jewel, the Fun
Couple, the Bonnie and Clyde of the animal world.
Magaracz was unarmed. Carl Gables would have, perhaps, a pocketful of poisoned hypodermic needles, and
even with one arm in a cast he was probably pretty quick
with a needle. *I hate shots.* The bride of Gables's heart
had her huge fangs, like sharpened stainless steel bana-
nas. *Can you feature it?* He featured it; at the end of the
feature Mrs. Magaracz's boy lay in several pieces at the
bottom of the stairs, his brown suit ruined.

Clearly this was a time for guile before physical
confrontation. The van's engine was running; the keys
were in it. Magaracz jumped in and drove quietly away.

Twenty-two

Ophelia was about to reveal to Kevin Mandelbaum the truth about her husband, that base act by whose commission he had sundered himself forever from the community of the civilized, when there was a sharp knock on Kevin's office door.

"Come in," said Kevin.

A huge cowboy stood in the door frame, his bulk filling it, his belly hanging over his belt, his big florid face framed by a furry sheepskin collar.

"Can we help you with something?" Kevin asked him.

"Sorry to bother you folks, but do you know anything about a gray Dodge van with Jersey plates, bars all over the windows? It's blocking me in. I'm supposed to take a load to Elizabeth and I can't get my rig out."

"No, I'm sorry, I don't."

The trucker sucked his teeth. "I don't know what to do then," he said.

Ophelia said, "Why don't you have the telephone operator page the van's owner?"

"Nobody answers the phones. I think the operator went home."

"That could be a problem," said Kevin.

"I need to get going right away," he said. "Mr. Baines said he wants this stuff out of here."

At these words Ophelia's face was suddenly flooded with understanding. She seemed to know who the man was, or what he was there to carry away. Her eyebrows went up. Elegant eyebrows. Did they grow that way naturally? Perfect adornments for a perfect face. She said, "Mr. Baines. Ah. Then perhaps Mr. Baines himself could help you."

"Yeah, if I could find his office," the man said. "This fuckin' place—excuse my French—"

"Oh, well," said Ophelia. "You're on the wrong level. You need to go up one more floor. Take the stairs right outside the door, there, and turn to your right." Why was she telling him that? It was all wrong. If he followed her directions the man was bound to become more hopelessly lost than ever.

"To the right," the man said. "Thanks." He closed the door and went away.

"Who was that?" said Kevin. "Why did you tell him to go upstairs and turn to the right? That's not the way to the main office."

"He's a trucker," she said. The brown eyes narrowed. "He's conspiring with Baines and my husband to do a very wicked thing. I thought perhaps . . ."

"I'm having trouble following you," Kevin admitted.

"Listen," she said. "I have to stop that man and his truck. Many lives are at stake." She stood up and put on her coat. "We'll talk later. I have to go." She picked up her purse.

"Wait!" he said. "Wait!" She was running down the hall. "I think I'm in love with you," he said, but she was gone.

When Dr. Carl Gables arrived at the top of the sub-basement stairway, short of breath, hefting a fifty-pound sack of monkey chow and a paper bag full of fresh fruit, he found that his new van was missing.

This was the one thing he had not figured on, that someone would steal his van here in suburban Princeton on a Friday night. Now he would have to change his plans. He hated that.

Perhaps the car. Heavily tranquilized, Jewel might sleep in the back seat. But it was so far from here to the circus in Florida where he had prepared a refuge for them. Nowhere for Jewel to eat, nowhere to answer the call of nature. His car could be traced. They would be followed and captured.

And time was growing short. He went back down the stairs to the lab, taking the chow and the fruit. He would have to think of something else.

Earl Hartson, the man in the cowboy outfit, continued to roam the halls, asking the few people he met whether they owned the gray van, and seeking the way to Jared Baines's office. At least he was on the right floor, now, according to the last person he asked. But everybody told him different. He could be here all night, walking up and down.

If Baines had stayed in the shipping department until all the crates were loaded, the way Earl told him to, then he could have signed the papers and the truck could have been halfway to Jersey City before the van's moron driver decided to park behind it. But no. These hard-chargers, they have to do three things at once, take five times as long. At this rate Faye would be asleep by the time he got home.

In the distance he saw a bright light. He hiked on, and came to the vestibule of Howard Strass's suite of offices. There was a smell of Chinese food.

Stretched out on the puffy pink-and-green rug in an uncomfortable looking position he found the mortal remains of Jared Baines, erstwhile hard-charger.

Kevin found Ophelia outdoors in one of the loading bays. It was raining, and yet she seemed to be searching a truck. She had a short length of hose and a galvanized bucket, probably scavenged from one of the maintenance closets.

"What are you doing?" he said.

"Go away, Kevin," she said. "Go back inside. Better yet, go home. I don't want you involved in this."

"What is it?"

"Go away. I'm going to have to go to jail for this. You don't want to be a part of it."

"Yes, I do. If you're a part of it, I want to be a part of it," he said. "Are you siphoning gas?"

She said, "Yes." She wore no hat; water was streaming off her hair.

"What for?" he said.

"I'm going to burn up this truckload of hivostatin. I warn you. Don't try to stop me."

"Darling, I don't want to stop you, I want to help you," he said. "Only tell me why we're doing this."

"Oh, Kevin! We're saving the world," she said, and burst into tears. He held her, massaging the sublime shoulder blades through her cloth coat.

"Yes," he murmured. "But from what?"

"Birth defects. Hivostatin causes birth defects. We have to destroy it before Jared Baines can ship it to Zaire. But why do you want to help me?"

"Because I love you," he said.

They kissed. Her lips were warm and soft, and salty with tears. Cold rain ran down their faces, down their necks. She pulled away from him and in a husky voice she said, "Do you know where they put the gas cap on one of these things?"

He knew. They drained out a bucket of gas and sloshed it around. Some of it spilled on the van that was parked behind the truck. It couldn't be helped. In any conflict you had to expect a few civilian casualties.

He rigged a makeshift fuse with a twist of paper, and lit it, and the two of them ran up the hill like mad people until they came to an evergreen bush. It was almost dry there. They snuggled together under its branches. WHUMP! went the gasoline.

They could feel the heat of the fire, even as far away as they were. "Maybe Porcpharm itself will catch fire," she said. "Maybe the whole thing will burn."

"Would you like that?" he said.

She said, "I've never been so excited."

"Kiss me again," he said.

Over the crackle and roar of the fire they heard

sirens, coming closer. The fire trucks already? No, it looked like the police.

"We should give ourselves up," she said.

"Not yet," he said.

Howard couldn't imagine what had become of Ophelia. He was passing the time while he waited for her in the parking lot by listening to a tape that gave him tips on sailing his boat. She had parked the Jaguar next to his Mercedes, so it was easy enough for him to wait there in the comfort of his own vehicle for her to turn up. He hoped she wasn't taking another crack at the animal labs. Whatever went on in that place would be moot when Supra Labs took over.

His tape began to play over again. What a long time she was taking. He could always go home, of course, but he wanted to talk to her now; there were so many things he needed to explain.

The sky was certainly growing bright. Was there a new shopping center—? But, no, it was something out behind the west wing. It was . . . it was fire.

He started the car, pulled out of his parking place, and raced around the west wing of the building, almost on two wheels. The flames were growing higher. With a bump the Mercedes was off the paving and rolling across the wet grass. As he rounded the corner he saw that it was not the building that burned, but the back end of a tractor trailer, and the van that was parked behind it. He braked and jumped out. Sirens wailed, closer and closer. The heat was intense.

At his feet there was a galvanized bucket and a hose. Who could have left these things here? He picked them up.

*   *   *

Carl Gables could hear the sirens, too. He sat at his desk by the door to the monkey labs, staring at his hands, contemplating his life.

This was not an activity that he ordinarily engaged in. Constant introspection was not one of his faults. But sometimes events force things on you, and right now Gables was forced to sit, an unaccustomed posture, and wonder how things had got so badly out of kilter.

He seemed to be living somebody else's life.

The pale green walls, the smells, the squeaks of blinded rabbits, all this seemed to him like a movie; presently it would stop and he would get up, throw away his popcorn box, put on his coat, and go find his car, to return to his real life waiting somewhere for him.

And what was that?

Caroline? The children? They seemed so strange to him. Somebody else's wife and children. Far away, perhaps in another city, were the people he should have been with, the lovers and companions destined to make him happy.

He had never met them. Now he never would.

How had this happened? When did he become an imposter in his own skin? Some other consciousness controlled him, some fever not himself, or else some parasitic space alien clamped to his neck. Wake up and leave the movie house.

He looked at Jewel, that beautiful creature of the long hair and liquid eyes. For a long time he used to think that with work and patience he could help her to be almost human—the lessons in sign language, tool use, grooming, toileting—but then he realized that this would not be an improvement, that humans were nothing to admire or emulate. He must become an ape.

Maybe that was his real life, an arboreal existence in the jungles of Borneo. He should have been a research scholar, secured a grant, emigrated. Too late. It was over now, over for them both. He would never let them take her.

He opened the door to Jewel's cage and took her warm, dry hand. Gently he embraced her shoulders and led her out. She smiled at him.

He took her to his office. They sat together on the desk. He held her hand, stroking the fur, tracing the simian crease with his forefinger. Her face was impossible to read. Like an infant, she seemed infinitely wise, perhaps because she was unable to speak and reveal her true mind. He could believe at times that she understood everything except the inevitability of death.

He had prepared two large doses of barbiturates, one for himself and one that he had put in a banana for Jewel. He signed, "Jewel eat," and offered the banana to her.

Nick Magaracz stepped out from behind a row of rat cages.

"I wouldn't eat that if I were you, sweetie," the detective said to Jewel. "Too much fruit is bad for little monkeys." He produced a chocolate bar and held it out to the ape. For a long moment she wavered, looking from Gables's face to Magaracz's and back again.

Then the traitorous bitch took the candy.

*   *   *

So then what happened?

Well, to begin with, the merger fell through. Supraordinate Laboratories backed out.

Then Ophelia went to her mother and told her everything, including the part where she had fallen in love with Kevin Mandelbaum and was going to leave Howard. Hester decided that Ophelia needed something to occupy her mind, so she put her in charge of Porcpharm.

Ophelia's first act as CEO was to fire Dr. Margaret Gagne. She sent her a telegram in the hospital. From there she went on to disband the entire research and development department, relying for future revenues almost entirely on Porcinox, their over-the-counter antacid, which was discovered to be of significant value in combating osteoporosis in postmenopausal women.

She personally found good homes for all the healthy animals in the monkey lab, and the rest she caused to be put out of their misery in the most humane way possible. Jewel was sold to an animal behaviorist at Princeton. Ophelia was assured his intentions were honorable.

As a result of the new corporate strategy, seventy-five percent of the Porcpharm employees had to be laid off.

Dr. Gagne, after making a complete recovery, went to work for Supraordinate Laboratories, where they doubled her salary and provided her with more complete and up-to-date research facilities than she had imagined in her wildest dreams.

Howard Strass is still out on bail. His case will come to trial some time next year. His lawyer feels confident that the attempted insurance fraud that forms the basis of the charges against him can be blamed on the unfortunate Jared Baines, who in his mad rise to the top neglected to fit himself up with a wife and children to defend his good name after his death.

Carl Gables was put in jail.

There never was any mention of the affair in any of the New Jersey papers. About a week after he stopped expecting to see the story someplace Magaracz went to the Thriftway to pick up some ricotta and hot sausage for Ethel. He was waiting at the checkout line when the headline on one of those national tabloids caught his eye:

VIVISECTIONIST SLEEPS WITH APE, KILLS BOSS TO HIDE AFFAIR

There was a picture of Carl Gables in handcuffs between two policemen, and a cut of Jewel's face in the upper corner. Magaracz supposed it was Jewel; actually all apes looked pretty much alike to him.

"Don't bother to buy it," the woman waiting in line in front of him advised. "The stories in there are never as good as the headlines."

He bought it anyway; he thought Ethel might want to see it.